RETURN TO

LIMESTONE

Life Is What It Is

JOHN DOUGLAS VALLEY

Valco **V** Books

Published 2018 by Valco Books

Cover Design by John Valley

Scripture quotations are taken from The Holy
Bible, New International Version (NIV) Copyright
1973, 1978, 1984 by International Bible Society.
Used by permission of Zondervan Publishing
House. All rights reserved.

Introduction by John Valley

Edited by Geneva Valley

Printed in the United States of America

This is a work of fiction. Although there are real persons, places and events throughout this novel, the basic storyline is fictional and should not be construed as factual. Any such persons, places or events mentioned in the basic storyline is not deliberately done so intentionally and is merely coincidental. This story is purely a figment of the author's imagination.

INTRODUCTION

Small town America, 1963! John F. Kennedy is the President of the United States. The Civil Rights movement is brewing heavily, especially after Dr. Martin Luther Kings' 'I Have a Dream' speech in Washington, DC. The 'English Music Invasion' is happening with The Beatles and The Rolling Stones leading the way.

America is high spirited, but also somewhat divided. The 'Hippie Movement' is getting underway, but there is deep distention in the South. The Cuban 'Bay of Pigs' crisis is over and President Kennedy has boldly proclaimed: *"The United States will put a man on the moon before the end of this decade."*

It is during this time that Thomas Chaimberbrook, now retired after a very distinguished military career, decides to move his family back to his old boyhood town, a small hamlet in upstate New York. Thomas' son, Tom, is a talented high school basketball player, who as a junior led his high school team in Indiana to a Conference Championship.

When Tom, now 6 feet 8 inches tall, enrolls at the local Limestone High School, it doesn't take long for him to be noticed!! Coach Marvin Smith is drooling over his teams' prospects for the season, knowing that he has the makings of a superstar on his hands.

Thomas, in the meantime, has been called to Washington, DC for an interview with FBI director J. Edgar Hoover. Hoover is impressed with Thomas' military career and feels like he would make a good agent for the Bureau. It is with this background that our story begins.............

PART ONE

September 1963

1

Tom Chaimberbrook was hurrying to his fifth period class. It was his first day in his new school, Limestone High, so he didn't want to be late. As he swung around the corner, *WHAM*! He had slammed into one of the teachers and knocked him down.

Tom held out his hand and helped the man to his feet. "Sorry sir, I was in a hurry to get to my next class", Tom explained.

As the man stood up, he looked up at Tom's 6 foot 8 inch frame and asked, "How's the weather up there, Partner?"

Tom was a little taken back at the remark at first, but then smiled and said, "Oh I've heard that one before a few times. The weather is just fine up here, how is it down there"?

The man smiled and said, "Just joking with you Partner, don't believe I've seen you around these parts before". Holding out his hand he said, "I'm Marvin Smith. My friends call me Marv, kids call me Coach".

"Coach"? Tom inquired.

"Yes, I am the basketball coach here at Limestone High. I noticed that you may be a good prospect. You do play basketball don't you"?

"Well, yes I have played a little here and there", Tom replied with a grin on his face.

"Don't believe I caught your name, Partner?" Smith asked.

"Tom Chaimberbrook", he answered, shaking the man's hand again.

"Tom Chaimberbrook!" Smith exclaimed with a curious look on his face. "I thought I seen a slight resemblance there. You are Thomas Chaimberbrook's son aren't you?"

"Why, yes sir, do you know my Dad?"

"Sure do, your Dad and I played basketball together many years ago".

"Seems like I do recall Dad talking about you before", Tom said.

"So tell me, how is your Dad? Last I heard he was in the Army making quite a name for himself."

"Well Dad is retired now"....CLAAANG! The bell interrupted Tom in mid-sentence. "Wow! I've got to run. I'm going to be late for class."

"Now hold on there Partner", Smith responded. "I'll walk you to your next class. That way you won't get charged with a tardy."

"Thank you sir, I appreciate that. I don't want to get started here on the wrong foot my first day".

"No problem", Smith said as he and Tom headed down the hallway. "So tell me more about your Dad. I sure would like to see him again."

"Well we moved back here to Limestone after Dad retired from the military and he is now in Washington, DC interviewing for a job with the FBI."

"I'm not surprised; your Dad was always a 'Go-getter'. Hope I get to see him when he gets back, maybe I'll see him at one of your games."

"You make it sound like I've already made the team", Tom said.

"Trust me, you have", Smith replied as they arrived at Tom's next classroom. Marv opened the door and walked in ahead of Tom.

"Hi George", Smith called out to the teacher. "Don't mark him tardy, he has been with me."

"No problem Marv we are just getting started. You must be Tom Chaimberbrook", the teacher replied. "I'm George Farmington, have a seat."

"Thank you sir", Tom said heading for a seat.

"Alright class, open your textbooks to page 23 as we prepare for today's lesson."

Meanwhile in Washington, D. C.   ......

Thomas Chaimberbrook was a bit nervous as he entered the Federal Bureau of Investigations building. He didn't know why he had been called into Washington by the FBI Chief, but he figured he would soon find out.

After looking at the directory in the entranceway, Thomas took the elevator to the fourth floor, turned left and walked to the fifth door on the right. There was the sign on the door: DIRECTOR-J.EDGAR HOOVER.

Thomas entered cautiously and seen the receptionist desk straight ahead. He slowly meandered up to the desk. "May I help you sir?" The lady at the desk asked.

"Ah, yes, I'm Thomas Chaimberbrook. I have an appointment with Mr. Hoover this morning."

"Yes, Mr. Hoover is expecting you. I'll buzz him." She reached for the intercom device and punched a button. "Mr. Chaimberbrook is here to see you Sir."

She was greeted with a gruff response, "Alright, send him in."

"Right this way sir." She led him across the room to another door, tapped lightly, and entered. "Mr. Hoover, this is Mr. Thomas Chaimberbrook."

As Thomas approached the desk of one of the most powerful men in Washington, DC, he was once again slightly nervous. He reached out his hand as Hoover arose to shake it. "Have a seat Chaimberbrook. I would like to discuss a possible position with the Bureau with you".

"Well that is a relief", Thomas said as he sat down. "I thought maybe I was being called in to be interrogated about something."

"Actually most of the interrogation has already been done on you", Hoover stated gruffly.

"Sir?" Thomas asked cautiously.

"Yes, I mean about the position. You see I have already done a thorough investigation into your background." Hoover unfolded a portfolio of the military accomplishments that Thomas had achieved.

"Very impressive military career", Hoover continued. "You were absolutely magnificent during the D-Day invasion in '44. Your bravery probably saved the lives of many of our soldiers that day. That was the first thing that I checked out, and all of it was substantiated by the Army Chief of staff."

"Many of our men died that day", Thomas stated, recalling vividly the horrors of that day almost two decades ago.

"Many more may have died if not for your bravery", Hoover came back. "You charged that hill where the German gunnery was raining down machine gun fire and killing off our troops by the dozens. You single handily popped a grenade into that bunker and took out that gunner, that no doubt saved many of our troops."

"God was with me that day", Thomas said softly.

"Speaking of God", Hoover continued, "After the war you were not only promoted from

Lieutenant to Captain, but then you became a Chaplain, and were able also minister too many of our service men. That proved especially helpful later when you were sent to lead a regiment of men in the Korean War. Many of our men were dying on the battlefield there as well. Your prayer support for our troops was very encouraging to those young men and gave them the stamina they needed to continue the fight."

"I do not like to brag about my military heroics, Sir", Thomas stated. "I appreciate all the flowers, but can we get to the point. Exactly what is the reason you called me in here for today?"

"That's what I really like about you Chaimberbrook, straight to the point. You are a man that likes to get right down to business."

"No need wasting each other's time, Sir. I know your time is valuable, frankly so is mine!"

"Alright, I'll tell you what I have in mind", Hoover retorted. "As you know we have had quite a disturbance lately in the South with all this Civil Rights nonsense going on. That King fellow has got all those people down there in Alabama all stirred up. He thinks those Negroes ought to have the right to vote and….."

"Excuse me, Sir, but technically they do have the right to vote", Thomas interrupted.

'Abraham Lincoln freed the slaves in this country in 1863 with the Emancipation Proclamation Act, and the 15th Amendment to the Constitution, in 1870, gave all men, born in this country, the right to vote. That includes African Americans, Sir!"

"I see you are really up on your history, Thomas", Hoover casually stated. "But the facts are that most of these, 'African Americans', as you put it, are just plain ignorant when it comes to political elections. They can't read, they can't write, they don't know anything about the history of our country, that is why we don't want them voting. They have no idea what our election process is all about."

"Perhaps we should educate them", Thomas bluntly stated.

"I can see you and I don't exactly agree on this issue", Hoover responded, a bit on edge.

"Let's get to the point, shall we? Why am I here?" Thomas was getting perturbed with Hoover's stalling.

"I want you to go down there to Alabama and see if you can find out just what gives with that King character. I don't like him stirring up trouble. He just gave a speech here in Washington last week that some 250,000 of his followers attended.

'Next thing you know he will want a meeting with the President! Kennedy doesn't have time for this nonsense. I want it stopped! That is what I want you to do. Find something on him that will take him out of the limelight before this gets out of hand."

"Well Sir, I do disagree with you on this issue", Thomas responded. "Frankly I believe Martin Luther King, Jr. and his followers do have the right to vote, and I believe their cause is just. I don't necessarily agree with the way they are going about it, but they are doing what is legal according to the First Amendment, which gives them the right of Freedom of Speech."

"What in hell is the matter with you Chaimberbrook", Hoover snapped at Thomas. "I am offering you an opportunity for a new career. You are still a young man, 40 years old. You would be a great asset to the department.

'I can assure you, this job would pay you much more than you earned in the military and probably more than you could make in civilian life."

"Frankly, I am not quite ready for any job right now", Thomas responded. "I have not been out of the military that long, and I am looking forward to spending some time with my family. I have a son who is a pretty good basketball player. He is a senior this year, and I have not been able to see many of his games.

'We've moved around a lot in the past few years. I want to settle down and watch my son play his final year in high school."

"You are passing up a golden opportunity, Thomas", Hoover came back, a little less harsh this time. "But I understand where you are coming from. I will still keep you in mind for any future assignments that may come up in the department. I wish you luck in whatever you decide to do. I hope your son has a good season this year."

"Thank you, Sir. I appreciate that. But I just don't think I am the man for the job you are looking for. I thank you for the interview, maybe some other time".

"Very well, Thomas. We'll leave it at that", Hoover said, holding out his hand.

Thomas shook the FBI Chief's hand, turned and walked out the door. *I wonder if I just did the right thing',* he thought as he headed for the elevator.

2

That evening at the dinner table……..

"Dad, I remember you used to talk about a guy named Marvin Smith. You used to play basketball with him back in your high school days?"

"Oh yes, Ole Marv and I were quite a team back then. He had a great set shot from about 25 to 30 feet out. Often times he would feed it into me in the middle, fake everybody out. Why do you ask?"

"Well I met 'Ole Marv' today; he is the basketball coach at Limestone High."

"Really; I often wondered what happened to Marv, lost track of him when I went into the service."

"Well he seemed to know who I was, especially after I told him my name. He said you are Thomas Chaimberbrook's son aren't you?"

"Wow, I sure would like to see Ole Marv again. I…."

"He said the same thing about you, Dad", Tom interrupted. Maybe we could have him over for supper some evening, and you two could get reacquainted."

"Hey, that's an excellent idea, Son. What do you think Martha?" Thomas asked turning to his wife.

"Sure, that would be great. You two could reminisce old times, and it would give Marv a chance to get to know Tom a little better", Martha answered."

"Well, he has already told me I have made the team", Tom spoke up.

"He told you that?" Thomas asked.

"Yup; I guess he figures I can play even though he has never seen me in action."

"Of course it doesn't hurt that you have had quite a bit of publicity already, and a few college scouts are looking at you." Thomas stated bluntly.

"I know", Tom replied. "But this is a small town, I don't know if Coach Smith has seen much of that publicity."

"Maybe not", Thomas said. "But Ole Marv sure can recognize basketball talent when he sees it. By the way, how is the football team looking this year?"

"I don't know. But there is a game at home this Saturday. Want to go?"

"Sure. Sounds like fun. Want to go Honey?" Thomas asked turning to his wife again.

"I haven't been to a football game in years." Martha stated. "Why not? Maybe we will get to see some of your old acquaintances."

"Great", Tom said arising from the table. "I've some homework to do, so if you will excuse me."

"Sure Son", Thomas said.

After Tom was out of hearing range Martha spoke up. "Alright, what happened in Washington today?" She asked.

"Well Mr. Hoover called me in to interview for a possible position with the FBI. It seems that he had already done quite a thorough background check on me. So I asked him to get to the point. Why was I there?"

"And"?

"After he told me what the job was about, I turned him down."

"You what, turned him down? Why on earth would you do that?"

"I didn't like what he had to offer."

"And just what did he have to offer?"

"He wanted me to go to Alabama and dig up some dirt on Martin Luther King Jr."

"What? Why would he want you to do that?"

"I don't think there is any love lost between Hoover and King. Hoover sees King as a threat, trying to stir up things, particularly in the South. King made it pretty clear in his 'I Have a Dream' speech last week that he is only asking for the government to recognize that African Americans have the same rights as any other American. And that includes the right to vote."

"Well I agree with Mr. King, they do have that right", Martha acknowledged.

"Hoover doesn't see it that way. He believes King's subornments are too illiterate to vote conscientiously. I suggested that we should educate them. He didn't like that idea. In fact, he got rather riled when I said that."

"Well you made the right choice. The gall of that man; I never would have guessed he was like that. He is supposed to be a highly respected man."

"He said he would keep me in mind if another position should open up. Not sure if I want to work for the FBI or not anyway. Money isn't everything. Besides I think a little time with my family would be nice."

"I'll say Amen to that", Martha said as she leaned over and kissed her husband.

Saturday morning at the game…….

"The old place sure has changed since I went to school here." Thomas explained, as the Chaimberbrook family entered the bleachers for the first football game of the season between Limestone High and Black Rock Central. The band was on the field and the cheerleaders were getting the crowd into the spirit.

"Hey Thomas, is that you old buddy", came a shout from just above where the family was sitting. Thomas turned around and there was his old friend Marv Smith!

"Marv, you old rascal you, how are you?" Thomas excitingly said as he rose to greet his old pal.

"Who is calling who an old rascal?" Marv came back, as he reached out to shake Thomas' hand and give him a hug.

Turning to his wife Marv said, "Honey, I would like to have you meet an old friend of mine, Thomas Chaimberbrook. Thomas this is my wife Sandy."

"Pleased to meet you Sandy", Thomas said. "How did you ever get stuck with this character?"

"Well it's a long story", Sandy said smiling. "I'll have to tell you about it sometime."

"Alright, I want you guys to meet my wife Martha", Thomas said.

He introduced Marv and Sandy to Martha and said, "I guess you already have met my son Tom."

"Sure have", Marv said. Turning to his wife, "Honey, this is the kid I have been telling you about." "

"All good I hope", Tom said extending his hand to Sandy, "Pleased to meet you Mrs. Smith."

"Hey, why don't you guys join us", Marv suggested. "There is room up here for all of us."

"Sure", Thomas said, "Then we can chat and catch up on some lost time."

"Well, I'm going to watch the game", Tom stated. "You guys go ahead. I think I see a couple of guys I know over there. I'm going to join them."

"You go ahead, Son", Thomas agreed. We'll catch up with you later."

Thomas and Marv sat down together, and Sandy and Martha sat side by side to get better acquainted.

"So tell me Marv", Thomas began, "how good is your basketball team going to be this year?"

"Well we have two seniors and two juniors coming back from last year's team, along with what I believe are three or four pretty good sophomore players, and a couple of freshmen. That is not counting Tom, of course."

"Tom seems pretty confident he has made the team, although I told him, maybe 'Coach' needs to see you play first."

"I don't need to see him play, Thomas", Marv said. "I know he can play. I've seen you in action, so I figure he is a 'chip of the old block'. Besides, I am well aware of your son's exploits. I can read you know! I've seen stories about him leading Mount Carmel to their Conference Championship last year. I suspect he has been scouted already by some colleges?"

"As a matter of fact, yes he has. I was a little hesitant about moving back here to Limestone at first; for fear that Tom might not get the publicity in a small school like he has gotten in larger schools. But Tom seemed eager to move here, and he said that he wanted to see the town I grew up in.

'You know, Marv, I have been gone from here almost 21 years. But I can tell you, I sure have seen a lot of changes since I've been gone."

"To be sure, Thomas", Marv offered. "So what about you my friend; what's in store for you now?"

"Not quite sure yet, going to take a little time off to try to figure things out".

"Tom told me you had an interview in Washington with the FBI. How did that go?"

"I decided not to take the job."

"Oh, should I ask why not?"

"I will tell you about it sometime. Right now let's watch the game. I see they are about ready to kickoff."

Limestone kicked off. Black Rock ran three plays and punted. After the runback, Limestone started first and ten at their own 38 yard line.

"You see that #12 down there at quarterback", Marv pointed down to the field. "That is Rick Jackson. Great athlete plays football, basketball, and baseball. He's only a junior. He will be one of our starting guards this season when basketball begins. Another one of our players is #23 over there at tight end. That's Nathan Boone. He is a junior also. At 6 foot 4 inches, he has been playing center for us, but I suspect I will move him to forward this year with Tom coming on board."

"I can see you are already getting your head into the season", Thomas smiled. "Come to think of it, you always did have your head into the game. You are a natural coach Marv. How did you land this job?"

"Well, I went to school at Georgia Tech down in Atlanta, played a little ball down there, and actually was an assistant coach for a couple of years. Then I met Sandy, we got married, and I had to find a REAL job! Ha! Ha!

'I got on as a draftsman for Coca-Cola to design new advertising slogans. It was a good job, made good money. Then I was up here five years ago visiting family, and I found out Limestone High School was interviewing for a basketball coach. I told Sandy, 'I am going to apply for that job just for the heck of it'. Low and behold, they hired me! We moved to Limestone, and we've been here since."

"Wow, quite a story. So now you are doing something you love."

"Absolutely, I have had a ball coaching these kids. And this year I feel like it is going to be something special!"

Just then the crowd came to their feet with a loud groan!! The game had been stopped and lying on the ground being attended to was Nathan Boone!

"What happened?" Marv asked someone in front of him.

"Nathan just made a sensational catch and was hit hard in mid-air. When he came down it looked like he twisted his ankle", the man in front of them informed.

After several minutes, attendants carried Boone off on a stretcher.

"Excuse me Thomas and ladies", Marv stated with deep concern. "I am going down to the locker room to check on Nathan. You guys enjoy the game. I'll be back."

3

The third quarter was halfway through before Marvin came back. In the meantime, Black Rock had taken a 24-7 lead and were driving once again.

"How is Nathan?" Thomas asked.

"Not good", Marv reported. "His ankle is broken. He will probably be out for the season. Hope he can get healed up before basketball starts. It is a tough loss for the football team though; especially for Rick Jackson. He and Nathan are not only teammates, but they are good friends as well."

"Sorry to hear that", Thomas said with remorse.

They sat almost in silence through the remainder of the game. Limestone managed to score once again in the fourth quarter, but it was offset by two more touchdowns by Black Rock. Final score: Black Rock Central 38, Limestone High 14.

After the game, as the crowd was leaving, Martha spoke up. "We would like to have you guys come over for supper some evening. When would be good for you?"

"I guess about anytime", Sandy said. "What do you have on your schedule Marv?"

"Well I have a staff meeting Wednesday evening, but about any other day would work."

"Great, how about Thursday evening", Martha asked.

"Thursday evening sounds good", Marv said.

"Great, looking forward to it", Thomas stated.

The men shook hands and the women hugged as they departed to the parking lot.

Thursday evening.......

"Honey, will you check those vegetables on the stove", Martha hollered out from the bedroom. "Make sure they aren't burning. You might need to add a little water to the carrots."

"Sure thing, Hon", Thomas answered. "Don't be so nervous. Everything will be fine".

"I don't want to have anything go wrong. This is kind of a special evening", Martha called back. "I really like Sandy and Marv. I don't want them to think I can't cook!"

"I doubt seriously they will get that impression", Thomas said. "You are an outstanding cook. Never heard anyone complain about your cooking yet!"

"Thank you, dear. I appreciate that. I just........." DING DONG! Martha was interrupted by the sound of the doorbell.

"I'll get it", Tom shouted heading for the door.

"Good evening, Coach and Mrs. Smith", Tom greeted the house guests. "Welcome. Please come on in".

"Thank you Tom", Marv said sniffing the air. "Boy something sure does smell good!"

"Can't beat Mom's cooking", Tom remarked, leading them into the living room.

Thomas approached from the kitchen. "Welcome friends", he smiled, holding out his hand to Marv. Giving Sandy a hug, he said "Have a seat. Martha will be out in a second, she is finishing putting her makeup on."

"Oh, Hi Marv and Sandy", Martha exclaimed coming out of the bedroom. Both stood and hugged Martha. "I'm just about finished in the kitchen. Hope you are hungry!"

"You bet", Marv spoke up. It smells delicious."

"Can I give you a hand", Sandy inquired as Martha headed towards the kitchen.

"Sure. Come on in here. We can let the men talk", Martha answered.

After the women exited the room, Thomas inquired, "How is Nathan Boone doing, Marv?"

"Well he is still in the hospital at Watertown. Doctor's had to do reinforcement surgery on his foot. Pretty bad break. They hope he can be released sometime this weekend, but the road to recovery is going to be a long one I'm afraid. It's going to take a lot of physical therapy before he'll be able to walk on his own again."

"I hate to hear that", Thomas stated.

"Alright, you guys", Martha called out. "Come and get it while it's hot!"

After everyone was seated around the table, Thomas said, "Let us pray.

'Heavenly Father, we gather here at our table now and give you thanks for this food and for your watch care over us today. We ask for your blessing upon this food. We thank you for this time that we can fellowship with an old friend and his wife. We thank you LORD for all of your blessings, because we know that all blessing come from you. We pray in JESUS name. AMEN.'

'Okay, everybody dig in!"

Everyone enjoyed the delicious meal of roast pork, mashed potatoes and gravy, carrots, broccoli, cauliflower, rolls and butter, topped off with apple pie for dessert! Light conversation accompanied the meal, the men talking mostly about the upcoming basketball season, and the women chatting about getting together to go shopping.

When the meal was over, the women cleaned up the table and set out to do the dishes. The men retired to the living room, and Tom went to his room to do some homework.

"That sure was a terrific meal", Marv said setting down in a nice reclining chair. "Your wife is an outstanding cook."

"Thank you, Marv. I have never heard anyone complain about her cooking. One of the blessings I have of being married to Martha."

"So tell me, Ole Buddy, How did you two meet?"

"Well, after I completed my basic training at Fort Dix, New Jersey, I was transferred to Fort Hood, Texas for advanced training. The war was getting pretty intense then, so the military was moving soldiers fast to get them ready for combat. Martha was a civilian working in the commissary on the base. We seem to hit it off the first time we met! We would see each other as much as possible during my training there, but I was only there for two months.

'I was deployed to Europe for battle. After six months of brutal combat, which saw 21 men in my unit killed, I was returned back, once again, to Fort Hood. As soon as I got there, I rushed to the commissary to see if Martha was still working there. Praise GOD she was! A week later we were married! I was not going to wait a moment longer!

'She has had to put up with a lot, being married to me. We have moved several times because of my military career. Tom was born in Texas in 1946 where I happened to be stationed at the time, and he has been exposed to several different schools. He has always done well academically, and has excelled in basketball since junior high. I am a blessed man!"

"Great story, Thomas", Marv said. "I am so glad you decided to come back to your roots. Now that Tom will be an important part of this season's team, I can't wait to get started!"

"Same Ole Marv, never stops thinking about basketball", Thomas stated. "I'll bet you still can hit that 25 foot set shot you used to make so often when we played together!"

"Set shots are a thing of the past, my friend. 'Jump shots' and 'dunks' are the big things now. But, in answer to your question, yes, I still can nail that shot fairly regular."

"You and I will have to play a little one-on-one sometime. What do you say?"

"I'm game. Think you are up to it?"

"It's been awhile since I've played", Thomas said. "But it would sure feel good to get back on the floor again."

"Ah, it's just like riding a bicycle", Marv came back. "Once you learn how to do it, you never forget.

'Look, Saturday morning there shouldn't be much going on at the school. The football team is playing away at Sauquoit Central, so let's sneak in a few shots in the gym. Say around 8 o'clock or so?"

"You're on. It will be good to see the old school again. I haven't been in that building since I graduated."

"You won't recognize the place", Marv said. There have been a lot of changes in the past two decades. Heck, there have been a lot of changes since I came back five years ago".

The women came back into the living room from the kitchen. After an hour or so of casual chat, Marv spoke up, "We better get going, Honey. Great catching up on old times tonight Thomas, and Martha, that was absolutely a scrumptious meal."

"It sure was", Sandy agreed, rising from the living room couch. "My turn next time to have you guys over. We have sure enjoyed this evening."

"I guess I will see you Saturday morning, Thomas?" Marv asked.

"You bet 8 o'clock. I'll be there."

4

Thomas and Tom pulled into the Limestone High School parking lot behind the school at precisely 8 o'clock Saturday morning. Marv's car was already parked there. "That rascal is probably already in the gym", Thomas said.

They got out of the car and walked into a door on the lower corridor. Walking up a flight of stairs Thomas remarked, "Boy, this old building sure has changed a lot."

"Wait until you see the gymnasium, Dad", Tom stated. "Bet it looks different than when you went to school here."

They arrived at the gym, and there was Marv taking shots from about 30 feet out. "I see you are getting a head start on me this morning", Thomas hollered out.

"Need all the practice I can get", Marv came back. "After all I am going against TWO Chaimberbrook's this morning, it looks like!"

"I am just an observer", Tom stated. "Here to watch two old pro's go at it."

"Far cry from old pro's, Son", Thomas said.

"What do you think of the new gymnasium, Thomas?" Marv asked.

"Wow, very impressive", Thomas said looking around. "When did they build this?"

"Four years ago. It went under construction right after my first year back. The old gym was in dire need for repair, and it was too small. So they built this new one. It seats about 1200 for basketball. The old one, you may recall, seated around 700."

"I like it", Thomas said with a smile. "So do I get a chance to warmup a bit before we start?"

"Of course", Marv said, grabbing a couple of more balls from the ball rack. "Here you go Tom; you can take some shots too."

Thomas warmed up for about five minutes, hitting about half of his shots. Meanwhile, Marv had his eye on Tom at the other end of the court, drilling shot after shot with amazing accuracy. A big smile came on his face as he watched a shooting clinic being displayed before his eyes.

"Well, I guess I'm ready", Thomas said, turning towards Marv watching his son. "Think he can play, Marv?" Thomas asked rather discreetly.

"He's a natural", Marv answered. "I knew it all along. He is a 'chip off the old block'."

"Well, let's see just what this 'old block' can do. Are you ready?"

"Alright, Partner, let's do it!"

Marv let Thomas take the ball out first. They jostled around a bit, then Thomas let go with a short shot about 10 feet out. Missed! Marv rebounded and put it up and in. "Try again, Buddy", Marv said.

Thomas took the ball out again. He dribbled around a little, and then SWOOSH; Marv stole the ball and drove in for a layup.

"I told you it's been awhile since I played", Thomas stated. "Here you take it out", he said, tossing the ball to Marv.

Marv took the ball out. Backing up about 10 feet, he let go from 30 feet out. SWISH! "I told you I can still nail that shot", Marv smiled.

"You are too much for me", Thomas said, shaking his head. "Maybe you need to play a round with Tom instead?"

"Well how about it Tom? Want to play a little one-on-one?" Marv shouted out.

"Sure", Tom called back.

The two squared off. Tom took the ball out first. Like lightning he drove around Marv and laid it up and in! Marv took the ball out. Cautiously dribbling to his left, he quickly switched to his right and drove to the basket. His shot was blocked by Tom, who pounced on the ball, pulled out to the foul strip, faked right and hooked left, off the backboard and in!

"Enough already!" Marv said, gasping for breath. "You don't have to prove anymore to me. You have made the team!"

"Thanks Coach", Tom said with a grin. "But I didn't even break a sweat!"

"Boy I sure did", Marv answered. Turning to Thomas he said "Can't wait for the season to start." Let's take a break Thomas. I need a drink", Marv said, heading for the drinking fountain just outside the gym door.

Thomas joined him, while Tom stayed in the gym continuing more shots. "You taught him well, Thomas", Marv smiled. "He has a great personality, not to mention his basketball talent."

"Well, he got his personality from his mother", Thomas came back. "And as far as his talent, he pretty much learned that on his own. I hate to admit it, but the fact is I have not seen Tom play a whole lot because of my military obligations. That is one reason I am not too anxious to go back to work for a while. I want to be able to enjoy watching him play his final year in high school."

"I can understand that", Marv said, as the two of them walked back in the gym and sat down on a lower section of bleachers. Watching Tom display his expertise at the other end, Marv asked, "Is that why you turned down the job in Washington?"

"Partially", Thomas answered, "But there was more to it than that. Hoover wanted me to go after Dr. King about what is going on with the civil rights movement. I didn't like his attitude towards Mr. King so I turned him down."

"Wow, not everybody would turn down a position with the FBI. I am sure it was a well-paying job."

"No doubt, we never got to that point of the conversation. But there will be something out there for me soon. I'm not worried about it"

"Ever thought about coaching?" Marv asked, out of the blue.

"What? You mean coaching, as in basketball?" Thomas seemed a little perplexed by the question.

"Of course, basketball, what else would I be talking about?"

"Knowing you, it could ONLY be basketball! You live it; it's the only sport you know."

"Well I suppose that's true, sure enough. But I asked, because I am getting to something."

"Like what?" Thomas asked curiously.

"Well you see I am the only paid basketball coach here at Limestone High. In fact I am only one of three coaches here that actually get paid! The others being football coach Norman Yandowski and baseball coach Bill Stanley.

'Now the school will not let me hire an assistant, because they haven't allowed for it in the budget. However, they will allow me to have a volunteer assistant, which means NO PAY! Think you might be interested in something like that?"

"Hum, interesting proposition, Marv", Thomas answered. "I'll have to give it some thought. Never did any coaching before."

"You know a lot about the game Thomas", Marv said, "Coaching is a lot of fun. You would have a ball with these kids. Not to mention, you would not only be able to watch Tom play, but could actually guide him along the way as well."

"I'll think about it, Marv. Need to talk it over with Martha and Tom also. He may not like the idea of his Dad coaching him."

"Nonsense!" Marv exclaimed. "I would bet he would love to have you coach him. You said yourself that you haven't spent much time with him on the basketball court. Now is your chance, Buddy!"

"Like I said, I'll give it some thought. A little prayer wouldn't hurt either!"

"Amen to that", Marv said. "Speaking of prayer, where are you guys going to church now?"

"We haven't really found a church yet, only been back in town a month. Do you have any suggestions?"

"Well, Sandy and I would love to have you join us this Sunday, if you would like!?" Marv said, half in a statement and half asking.

"I will talk it over with Martha; see what she has in mind. It sounds good to me!" Thomas said. "Oh, wait a minute. We can't this Sunday. We are going down to Cortland to visit my cousin. But I will talk with Martha about it, and maybe we can go next Sunday."

"Alright, we will leave it at that then. And pray about my proposal, Thomas. I'd love to have you as my assistant."

"I will", Thomas answered, getting up to leave. "I'll let you know something in a couple of days."

Sunday morning, on the way to Cortland.........

"Dad, do you think Coach was impressed with what he saw yesterday?" Tom asked from the back seat.

"Was he impressed? He thinks you are a natural! I don't believe he has had the opportunity to coach a player quite like you before."

"Well, I am not used to playing at a small school. I hope I don't deprive someone else from an opportunity to play."

"That's mighty thoughtful of you Son, but Marv is really looking forward to this season. He sees a rare chance for Limestone High to shine in basketball this year. It has been a long time since they have had a contending basketball team. This could be the year that changes."

"Yeah, I talked with Larry Jones the other day. He is a senior that has played for the past two years. He said they have had some fairly good teams, but just couldn't quite play with the bigger schools. Schools like Palmdale High and East Damon; they are lot bigger than Limestone."

"Well that's true, but the old saying is, 'The Bigger They Are, the Harder They Fall'".

"You sound a lot like a coach, Dad."

"That leads me to another subject", Thomas inserted. "Marv has asked me to be his assistant this season. What do you think of that?"

"Oh Thomas, that is wonderful!" Martha exclaimed. "What a great opportunity. I am so excited for you!"

"What do you think, Son?" Thomas asked.

"I think it is great! The old ONE-TWO punch back together. Smith and Chaimberbrook, soars again!" Tom cracked.

"Oh Honey, a new job just when we need it!" Martha sang out.

"Well, I would prefer to call it an opportunity rather than a job", Thomas stated bluntly. "The pay isn't all that good."

"Anything will help bolster your retirement from the Army", Martha said smiling. "Besides, it is only a temporary position and I'm sure you will enjoy it."

"Enjoy it, yes; bolster my retirement, no!" Thomas said frankly.

"What do you mean by that?" Martha inquired.

"It is a volunteer position. NO PAY! School didn't allow for it in their budget."

"Oh, I see", Martha's tone changing rapidly.

"That is why I believe we need to pray about it", Thomas stated. "Something else came up in our conversation yesterday. Marv wanted to know if we would like to go to church with them some Sunday!?"

"We really do need to get back in church, Thomas", Martha said. "Yes, I would like to go with them to see what the church is like."

"Tom, would you like to go with us?" Thomas asked his son.

"That is another thing that Larry Jones and I talked about. He asked me if I would like to go to church with him sometime. I told him I'd ask you, Dad. Do you mind?"

"Not at all, Son; I am delighted that you have met someone that goes to church. Most teenagers aren't very much interested."

"Larry is a real neat guy, Dad. We have a couple of classes together. He loves basketball, and the LORD. We have become good friends already."

"That's great, Son. Well I see we are almost here; just around the next curve is Walter's house."

5

Monday morning after breakfast, Thomas spoke up, "I am going to take a ride around town. I need a little time to ponder this coaching position that Marv has offered me. Do you need me to pick up anything at the grocery store?"

"I can't think of anything offhand", Martha answered. "You go ahead; I have some cleaning to do. Take your time, and don't worry; whatever you decide, I am willing to go along with your judgement."

"Thank you, Hon", Thomas said, as he kissed his wife and headed out the door.

Thomas drove around for about an hour thinking and praying about whether or not he should take Marv up on his proposal. He pulled up in front of 'Hank's Diner', a local coffee shop, parked the car and walked in. Sitting down at the counter, he ordered a cup of coffee. A couple of minutes later, someone tapped him on the shoulder.

"If I am not mistaken, I believe you are Thomas Chaimberbrook!" A man stated, quite sure of himself.

Thomas turned around and said, "Why yes, I am. Do I know you?" He asked with a curious look on his face.

"You probably don't recognize me, Thomas. It has been 20 years plus since we last seen each other! But I sure did recognize you!"

"I am sorry, but I can't place who you are", Thomas bluntly stated.

"Ralph Stevens. Does the name ring a bell?"

"Well I'll be", Thomas said, recognizing his old schoolmate. "Now I do remember. Class of '41; we graduated together!"

"That's right, and I was even on the basketball team with you, although I was pretty much of a bench warmer, didn't play much."

"I remember, but I also recall a game where you sank two critical foul shots against Corker Ville that won the game for us!"

"Ah yes. That was a long time ago. Highlight of my career I guess", Stevens said laughing. "Now you Thomas, you were something else. You and Marvin Smith were players back in those days. Marvin had a great set shot from around 30 feet, I remember".

"Well, I can tell you, he still can nail that shot. He is the coach here at Limestone High now."

"Yes, I know. I see Marvin every now and then. Don't have any kids in school anymore, so I haven't seen any games in the past few years."

"Well you need to come to a few this year, Ralph. I have got a feeling that Limestone is going to be pretty good."

"Really? There hasn't been a good team here in quite a while. It is tough for Limestone to compete since they realigned the conference. Most of the schools are larger, so obviously they generally have bigger, faster, more skilled kids."

"That may change this year. My son is going to be playing here, and frankly he is a pretty good player. As a matter of fact, Marvin has even asked me to be his assistant."

"Well good for you Thomas. I just might have to take in some games this year. Sure would be nice to see a winner in this town again."

"Of course I haven't accepted the job yet, I am still thinking about it."

"It's a no brainer, Thomas. Go for it! "

"I just might do that", Thomas said, dropping some change on the counter. "Good to see you again Ralph. Hope to see you at a game sometime."

"You can count on it; I am looking forward to it. See you around Thomas."

Later that evening……….

"Well I guess I will take that coaching job Marv offered me", Thomas stated, as the family sat down for supper. "I hope you will feel comfortable with that, Son."

"Yes!" Tom exclaimed. "I was hoping you would do it, Dad."

"Martha, are you okay with that too?"

"I told you this morning, whatever you decide I'm with you. It will be exciting watching both my son and my husband in action. And by the way, Sandy and I are going on a shopping trip tomorrow. She is going to pick me up around 9 o'clock in the morning."

"Good, it will give you two a chance to get better acquainted."

"We are going to Watertown. A new shopping center just opened there and we are going to check it out."

"Okay. I guess I will see if I can get with Marv for lunch. I'll let him know my decision. That should put him in a good mood."

Later that evening Thomas gave Marv a call and arranged for a lunch get together the next day.

Tuesday morning………..

"Well, there is Sandy pulling into the driveway now", Martha said looking out the window. "She obviously believes in being on time", looking at the clock on the wall, which read 8:45.

"Come on in Sandy", Martha said raising her voice as she opened the door. "Cup of coffee?" she asked.

"Maybe a half a cup", Sandy answered getting out of the car. "I've already had a couple of cups this morning."

"Good morning Sandy", Thomas greeted Sandy as she entered the front door. "Coffee is hot and ready."

"Just a little for me Thomas, already had my usual dosage this morning!"

Thomas, Martha, and Sandy chatted for a few minutes. Thomas let Sandy know that he was going to accept Marv's offer.

"I kind of figured that was what you two were getting together for lunch about", Sandy said.

"Well you guys have fun", Martha said getting up from the table. "We gals are going shopping! Come on Sandy let's get rolling!"

"Alright, Honey. See you later", Thomas stated.

On the way to Watertown………

"I am so happy you and Thomas moved back here to Limestone, Martha. Marv talked about Thomas often, they were good friends back in their teenage years. Now they are back in their old stomping grounds once again. Amazing how things work out, isn't it?"

"Yes, God has a way of surprising you doesn't he?" Martha answered. "Thomas has wanted to come back here for a long time, but we never could until he retired from the Army. Even then he was a little hesitant, because he didn't know how Tom would react, playing in small school. He has always been in a larger school all this time, but he said he wanted to come back here where Thomas was born. He wanted to see where his father spent his younger days."

"Just the opposite when Marv and I moved here five years ago", Sandy stated. Our daughter was very unhappy about moving to a small town like Limestone."

"Daughter!?" Martha exclaimed. "I didn't know you and Marv had any children!"

"Well, I guess that is one subject that we haven't talked about yet, Martha. Yes, we have a daughter. Her name is Lori, and she is now a freshman at Georgia Tech in Atlanta, same place Marv went to college."

"Wow! How about that? So she didn't like small town America, huh?"

"No she did not! She finished high school here, but she wanted to go to college where several of her old friends were. She was accepted at Tech and she says she is doing well.

'Haven't seen her since she left about a month ago, but she will be home for Thanksgiving. You will get to meet her then."

"Wow, that's great! I can't wait to meet her. Thomas never mentioned anything about you two having any children. I'm surprised he hasn't told me that before."

"He probably didn't know it either. You know when he and Marv get together; the topic of conversation is usually basketball. I don't think they talk much about personal things. It's a man thing, you know?"

"Yes, you're right! Men seem more interested in sports, the weather, and politics than personal stuff. So tell me, what is your daughter studying at Georgia Tech, and don't tell me she went there to play basketball."

"No way", Sandy exclaimed. "Surprisingly, Lori never really had much interest in basketball, much to the disappointment of Marv. She did play some softball at Limestone High, but basketball was not her thing.

'In answer to your question, Lori is studying computer science. She believes that computers are going to be the wave of the future. At least that is what she thinks she wants to do for now. That will probably change as she gets a little older, but she is a pretty smart girl. She is way beyond her age as far as maturity is concerned.

'Well, we are almost here", Sandy stated as she turned down Arsenal Street. "There it is, the new Watertown Shopping Extravaganza Adventure!"

"Wow!" Martha exclaimed. "We can shop 'till we drop! Where are we going first?"

"Let's see what Sears & Roebuck has to offer right over there", Sandy said pointing.

"Sounds good to me; let's do it!"

6

Meanwhile back in Limestone......... ⚹

"Thomas, old buddy that is the best news I've heard today!" Marv said reacting to Thomas telling him he would take the position as his assistant. "I am telling you, we are going to have a ball this year. This is shaping up to be the best team I've had since being here. Heck, it's the best team they have had at this school in years. We are going places this year, you watch and see!"

"You make it sound so exciting Marv", Thomas smiled. "Then again, I have to remember, basketball is your life."

"Yep, sure is. I'm in Hog Heaven doing this, Thomas. Best job I've ever had! I am telling you, you will get the fever too once we get started!"

"So when do we get started?" Thomas asked.

"Have to wait until November 1st to officially start team practice, according to New York State rules. But I encourage the kids to go ahead and practice on their own to get in shape for the season. Especially, running and working out with the weights. This will help get your body conditioned to the fast pace the game has now adjusted to, much faster now than when we played Thomas."

"Oh yes, I know. I like the new style of play. Players and fans get a lot more excitement out of the game now. And you are right; it takes a lot more stamina to play now. I guess I am not in very good shape to play now. I need to work out myself!"

"Can I get you gentlemen anything else?" the waitress asked stopping by their booth.

"Yes, I would like a cup of coffee" Thomas spoke up. "How about you Marv?"

"Sure, I'll have a cup too."

"Coming right up" the waitress replied. "I'll be right back."

"Well, this old place has not changed a whole lot" Thomas stated. "I remember 'Hank's Diner' was here over twenty years ago when I lived here."

"Yep, this place has been here since we were kids. They have made a few changes here and there, and painted several times, but it is pretty much the same. It's still a local hangout with good food and hospitality."

"Yeah, I bumped into Ralph Stevens here a couple of days ago. I didn't recognize him until he introduced himself to me. It has been a long time since I've seen ole Ralph."

"Ah yes, Ralph is still around. Never did leave Limestone. He has had a lot of tragedy in his life. Poor fellow just seems to be in a daze half the time."

"Really!" Thomas exclaimed. "He never mentioned anything about that when we were talking. Of course, we didn't talk very long. So what kind of tragedy are we talking about here?"

"Here you go gentlemen", the waitress returned with their coffee. "Piping hot, freshly made, enjoy!"

"Thank you", Marv said as she turned away. "Well, Ralph lost his mother several years back, and then about eight years ago he and his wife divorced. I don't think he ever recovered from that. He started drinking heavily for quite a while, but he finally quit. Then just two years ago, he lost his son in a very bad car accident down in Syracuse. Four young men were drag racing on Salina Street and collided with each other. All four of them were killed. Ralph's son was one of them. He was only 17 years old"

"I am so sorry to hear this Marv. I didn't know anything about that. Poor guy; sounds like he really needs a friend. I mentioned to him that I might be coaching with you this year and he seemed to brighten up a little. He said he had not been to a game in several years."

"No, I haven't seen Ralph at a game since I've been coaching here. He pretty much stays to himself. I try to befriend him when I can, but he is sort of resolute.

'Nice guy, though, doesn't bother anybody. I feel sorry for him. Wish there was something I could do to help him get over all he has been through."

"Yeah, maybe there is", Thomas said with a concerned look on his face.

"Oh, what have you got in mind?" Marv asked curiously.

"Well you asked Martha and me if we would like to go to church with you. And we have decided we will go with you this Sunday. If you don't mind, I would like to ask Ralph if he would go with us also."

"Great idea Thomas; I don't know if he will accept, but it wouldn't hurt to ask. He is generally around here at lunch time, but I haven't seen him today; must have had something else going on."

"Yeah, I'll see if I can get in touch with him" Thomas said rising from his seat. "Great lunch, Marv; keep me posted on the basketball team. I'll see you Sunday."

Thomas paid for both of their lunches, and as they were walking out the door, Ralph Stevens was walking in. Both Thomas and Marv greeted him, and then Thomas spoke up…….

"Hey Ralph, if you got a minute I'd like to talk with you about something."

"Sure Thomas, I'm in no hurry. Come in and have a cup of coffee with me."

"I will let you two gentlemen chat", Marv said. "I have to get back to work; got a class in five minutes, got to run."

Marv left and Thomas went back into the diner with Ralph. After they got seated Ralph ordered a burger and fries, Thomas ordered another cup of coffee.

"Well, what's on your mind Thomas?" Ralph asked.

"Ralph, Marv has been telling me what has happened with you in recent years. I am so sorry. I didn't know any of this until Marv told me. I feel like I sort of cut you off the other day, and I do apologize for that. It was purely unintentional, I assure you."

"No need to apologize Thomas, you had no way of knowing. Besides, I would just as soon not be reminded of what has happened. It is still hard for me to bear."

"I certainly understand that Ralph. I would like to be your friend, if you would allow me to be. Might I ask you a sort of personal question?"

"Sure Thomas. And I have always considered you a friend, even though we have been apart for many years. Our lives just went in different directions."

"That is true Ralph; look, I was wondering if you have any church affiliation?"

"No, I'm afraid not. I quit going to church a long time ago. I guess I resented GOD for what has happened to me! Yes, I know that is pretty stupid. But I was very bitter for a long time. LIFE IS WHAT IT IS, Thomas. I have finally learned to accept it."

"Ralph, would you consider going to church with me this Sunday? I would love to have you meet my wife and son. We are going with Marv and his wife. You know them and that should make you feel more comfortable about it. What do you say?"

"I don't know, Thomas. It has been a long time; I'll have to think about it. Check with me in a couple of days, I'll let you know then."

"Very well, we will leave it at that. Let's have lunch Friday. Okay?"

"Alright, meet me here around noon time."

"See you then", Thomas said dismissing himself. He walked over to the checkout and paid for Ralph's lunch on his way out the door.

Later that evening, at the dinner table……

"Well, how did it go with you and Sandy today?" Thomas asked Martha.

"Wonderful! Thomas that new shopping center is fantastic!" Martha exclaimed. "They have got all kinds of stores there; including sporting goods stores and men's clothing stores that even you would be impressed"

"Mom, would you pass the potatoes please?" Tom asked.

"Oh sorry Honey" Martha apologized as she passed the potatoes. "I am so excited I forgot what I was doing! Seriously Thomas, you will have to go with me sometime soon. You will be amazed at what is there."

"I am glad you enjoyed your little shopping spree; and I will consider going with you sometime." Thomas answered. "And speak about getting excited; Marv got all excited when I told him I would take the assistant position. I tell you he is so pumped up. He can't wait for the season to get underway."

"So you are going to coach me, Dad? Cool!" Tom spoke up.

"Well, keep in mind, Son, Marv is the head coach; I am just his assistant."

"Wow, that's great, Dad. You'll love coaching, and you will have a 'Ring Side' seat to watch all the action."

"Thank you for your confidence in me, Son. I will try to live up to your expectations."

"You will, Dad. You are going to be a great coach, I just know it! Oh, by the way, this is changing the subject a little, but Larry Jones asked me again today about going to church with him Sunday. Is it okay, Dad?"

"But of course, Son. We are going with Marv and Sandy, so you go ahead and go with your new friend. I am looking forward to meeting him."

"Thanks, Dad. And you will be meeting him soon when basketball season starts."

"Indeed I will", Thomas stated casually. Turning to Martha he said, "Oh, Ah, I hope you don't mind Honey, I have invited an old friend of mine to join us this Sunday as well."

"Oh, and whom might that be?" Martha asked.

"Well, you don't know him, but I ran across him at 'Hank's Diner' the other day. His name is Ralph Stevens; we played basketball together when I was in high school here many years ago. Poor guy has had a lot of problems in his life and has been out of church for quite some time. I asked him to join us this Sunday; he is supposed to let me know Friday whether or not he is going. I hope he does."

"Sure. May he find solace in the LORD! I'm looking forward to getting back in church. Do you realize, Thomas, it has been over three months since we have been in church?"

"Yes, I am ashamed to admit it. But hopefully that is all going to change this Sunday. Marv is going to pick us up around 10:30, service starts at 11:00."

"Great. Well I have some other news for you that may surprise you!"

"Excuse me, Dad, Mom; I have some homework I need to get at", Tom spoke up, rising from the table.

"Certainly, Son, you go ahead", Thomas stated. "So what is this surprising news that you have, Honey?"

"Did you know that Marv and Sandy have a daughter?"

"What? I don't think so, Hon; Marv has never said anything to me about him and Sandy having any children!?"

"Well Sandy informed me today that they have a daughter. She is a freshman at Georgia Tech."

"You have got to be kidding me! Why hasn't Marv ever mentioned this to me before?"

"Could it be because all you guys ever talk about is basketball?"

"Point well taken, I'll admit."

"Sandy showed me a picture of her; she is beautiful, Thomas. And she will be home for Thanksgiving, so we will get to meet her!"

"You sound pretty excited about this, Hon; so what is the big deal?"

"Tom, of course, that is the big deal!" Martha answered.

"What? Are you trying to play matchmaker for our son?"

"That is exactly what I may be trying to do, my dear. She would be a wonderful match for Tom. I think they would get along just fine."

"Martha, you have not even met this girl yet, and you don't know anything about her. What makes you think she would be a great match for Tom?"

"I just know it, Thomas. Call it 'a woman's intuition'; I just have a feeling they are going to click!"

"Easy, Martha; let's wait and see how things work out before you try matching the two of them up. Okay?"

"Alright, Thomas; but I know I'm right. You just wait and see!"

7

Thomas pulled up in front of 'Hank's Diner' at exactly 12:00 noon Friday. He parked the car and walked in, looking around for Ralph. Not seeing him, he took seat at the counter and ordered a cup of coffee.

"Have you seen Ralph Stevens in here today?" Thomas asked the waitress.

"No, not yet; but he comes in about this time fairly regularly", the waitress answered.

Thomas waited another 15 minutes and Ralph still hadn't shown. He was beginning to wonder if Ralph had forgotten their luncheon engagement. Ten minutes later he decided to leave. Dropping a dime on the counter, he said "If Ralph shows up here, tell him I was here but figured something came up and he couldn't meet with me today."

"Okay, I'll tell him", the waitress answered.

Just as Thomas got to his car, Ralph pulled up.

"Thomas, I'm sorry about being late", Ralph apologized. "I'll be danged if I didn't have a flat tire just as I was about to leave for here; had to put my spare on before I could move. Dropped the flat off over at 'Fred's Tire Shop' on the way over here, that's why I'm late."

"No problem, Ralph; I was just a little worried about you. Let's grab some lunch, what do you say?"

"I say, let's eat!"

They entered the coffee shop and found an empty table over to one side and took a seat. A waitress came over and handed them a couple of menus, and said, "What can I get you gentlemen to drink today?"

"Coffee for me", Thomas spoke up.

"I'll take the same", Ralph said. "And I'll have my usual, burger and fries."

"I will try the club sandwich and fries", Thomas said.

"Coming right up Gents", the waitress said. "I'll be right back."

A minute later she was back with the coffee.

"Thanks Kathy", Ralph said.

"Your food will be up in a jiff", Kathy replied.

"I guess you know some of these waitresses pretty well, huh Ralph?"

"Well I come in here a lot, so I have got to know some of them; at least their names. It's a friendly place and the food is good. I enjoy coming here."

"Yeah, 'Hank's' hasn't changed a whole lot over the years. Remember the 'Good Old Days', Ralph. We used to hangout here when we were teenagers."

"Oh yes, I remember. Seems like a long time ago, Thomas. A lot of water has gone over the dam since those days."

"Sure has my friend. So tell me, what have you decided about going to church with us Sunday?"

"Here you are gentlemen", the waitress interrupted as she brought their meals. "And here is the ketchup bottle as well. Can I get you anything else right now?"

"I guess that will be all for now", Thomas said. "Thank you."

"You are welcome", she said turning away.

"Well, you know, Thomas, I have been thinking about that a lot since we talked the other day. And I think maybe it is about time I got back in church. I believe I'll take you up on your offer,"

"That is great, Ralph!" Thomas exclaimed. "I am so glad you accepted. Now we are going with Marv and Sandy, and they are going to pick us up around 10:30, so we should be at you house about 10: 35 or so."

"I'll be ready, Thomas. You know, I am so glad you decided to come back to Limestone. It's been kind of lonely around this old town for a long time. Maybe things are starting to look a little brighter."

"Things always look brighter when you look upon the LORD, Ralph!"

"Yes, I know. And knowing we might have a good basketball team this year is quite a change as well; when do you get started, Thomas?"

"First practice is November 1st. First game is November 8th against Adirondack Parochial."

"Whoa; that is a tough opener; generally those Catholic schools are pretty good."

"I know. But it will be a good test right off the bat to see just how good we are."

"I'll be there. That should be a good game."

"You come to the games, Ralph, and I will see if I can get you seated right behind the bench where Marv's wife and my wife will sit. It will put you right into the game!"

"Thanks, Thomas; I never have sat that close without actually being in the game myself. Ha! Ha!"

"About time you did then. Waitress! Check please."

Thomas payed for both of their lunches and they headed out the door. As they reached their automobiles Thomas said, "I'll see you Sunday, Ralph; somewhere around 10:35 or there about."

"Looking forward to it; see you then", Ralph answered back.

Sunday Morning……….

"10:15 Dear; Marv and Sandy will be here soon." Thomas was calling out to Martha.

"I am almost ready", Martha answered back from the bedroom. "Just a little dab of makeup and I will be done."

"What time did you say your friend was picking you up Tom?" Thomas asked his son.

"He should be here right around the time you guys leave, Dad."

"Okay, well I guess we will see you later on after church then. I think I hear a car pulling into the driveway right now. Yup, it's Marv and Sandy. They are here, Martha!"

"Alright, I am ready. Right on time; Sandy and Marv are very punctual! See you later, Honey", Martha said giving Tom a hug and a kiss.

Marv backed out of the driveway and headed down the road. Thomas spoke up, "I never even gave it a thought to ask Ralph where he lived. I just took it for granted that you know, Marv?"

"Oh yeah; he lives out on North Road, about five minutes from here. Glad you convinced him to come with us today, Thomas"

"I didn't try to convince him really; I just asked him if he would consider going with us and he thought about it for a while, and decided to go."

"Great! Ralph lives kind of a lonely life; I hope this helps to give him some confidence to open up a little to other people."

"Yeah, he seemed pretty relaxed around me. Says he is looking forward to basketball season. I thought maybe we could arrange for him to sit right behind the bench. Suppose you can pull that one off, Marv?"

"No problem. I'll take care of it. Ah, here we are; that gray house over there on the left", Marv said pointing.

Marv pulled into the driveway and Ralph came out immediately.

"Good morning Ralph", Marv greeted him. "Glad you are joining us today."

"Good morning Marv, Sandy, Thomas", Ralph said climbing into the back seat."

"Ralph, I would like you to meet my wife Martha", Thomas said as Ralph got seated. "My son, Tom, is going to church with a friend of his today, so I guess you will meet him at another time."

"Pleased to meet you, Martha", Ralph answered. I should have known Thomas would pick a lovely thing like you."

"Well, thank you, Ralph", Martha answered. "I will accept that as a compliment."

They arrived at the church, parked and walked in. A fairly large crowd was gathered around in the lobby chatting; some were making their way into the main sanctuary. Marv introduced Thomas, Martha and Ralph to several people he knew. Just as they were about to enter the sanctuary, a voice called out.....

"Hey Dad! It's me!"

Thomas turned around and there was his son standing there with another young man and what appeared to be his parents.

"Well, I'll be", Thomas spoke out in surprise. "So your friend goes to this church too?"

"It seems that way", Tom answered. "Dad, Mom, I would like you to meet my friend Larry Jones and these are his parents."

"So pleased to meet you Larry", Thomas said shaking the young man's hand. Then reaching to shake the father's hand he said, "Thomas Chaimberbrook, Sir, and this is my wife Martha."

"It is a pleasure, Thomas", the man said, shaking Thomas's hand. "Lawrence Jones and this is my wife Irene."

Just then the music started inside the sanctuary. "Guess we had better find a seat." Marv spoke up. "We can all talk later".

The three couples sat together, with Larry, Tom and Ralph seated behind them. The congregation sang a couple of hymns, and then the assistant pastor made a few announcements before a prayer to prepare the people for the message. The choir then sang the anthem song before the pastor entered the pulpit.

"Today we are going to continue our study of the Sermon on the Mount." The pastor began. "Please turn your Bibles to the seventh chapter of Matthew and follow along with me as I read from God's Holy Word, beginning in verse 13."

Ralph reached for a pew Bible, but was having trouble finding the scripture. "Here let me help you, Sir", Tom volunteered, turning right to the passage.

"Thank you Tom", Ralph replied. "I am a little rusty at this."

"Your welcome, Sir", Tom said turning his attention back to the pastor.

"These are the words of our LORD", the pastor began.

"Enter through the narrow gate. For wide is the gate and broad is the road that leads to destruction, and many enter through it. But small is the gate and narrow is the road that leads to life and only a few find it."   Mat. 7:13-14

"Now, let's compare this to what the Psalmist says in Psalm one. Keep in mind these words were written almost 1000 years before the birth of our LORD Jesus Christ. The Psalmist writes:

Blessed is the man who does not walk in the counsel of the wicked or stand in the way of sinners or sit in the seat of mockers. But his delight is in the law of the Lord, and on his law he meditates day and night. He is like a tree planted by streams of water, which yields its fruit in season and whose leaf does not wither. Whatever he does prospers. Not so the wicked! They are like chaff that the wind blows away. Therefore the wicked will not stand in the judgement, nor sinners in the assembly of the righteous. For the Lord watches over the way of the righteous, but the way of the wicked will perish.   Psalm 1:1-6

"My message today", the pastor continued, "is entitled 'Which Road Are YOU On?' Both the Psalmist and our LORD make it very clear; there is only one WAY to eternal life!"

The pastor went on to preach a powerful message about salvation. He concluded by saying, "Jesus says in John 14:6":

"I am the way and the truth and the life. No man comes to the Father except through me."

"Again I ask you; Which Road Are YOU On? Please stand for the benediction"

After the service, Marv introduced his friends to the pastor. "Pastor Greg Simmons, I would like you to meet my friends Thomas and Martha Chaimberbrook and their son Tom. And this here is an old friend of mine, Ralph Stevens", Marv said wrapping his arm around Ralph's neck.

"Pleased to meet you pastor", Thomas said holding out his hand.

"Always a pleasure to meet new people in God's house", Pastor Greg said as he shook both Thomas' and Ralph's hand. "Please come back and join us again soon".

"Thank you Sir, we just might do that", Thomas stated.

The group all got together at 'Tiffany's Restaurant' for lunch. After everyone had placed their order, the conversation immediately turned to basketball. Marv turned to Larry and asked, "Well have you been working out to get into shape for the season?"

"Oh, yes Sir Coach. I've been running a couple of miles every day and working out with the weights in the weight room. Tom and I are ready to go, aren't we Tom?"

"You bet! Can't wait to get started", Tom answered.

"That's all Larry has been talking about since he and Tom became friends", Lawrence spoke up. "Looks like we may have a pretty good team this year; that right Marv?"

"Yup; boy am I excited!" Marv answered. "I believe this will be the best team I've had since I have been here. November 1st can't roll around soon enough to suite me!"

"Tell me, how is Nathan Boone coming along from his football injury?" Lawrence inquired.

"Well, he is improving", Marv answered. "But it will be a while before he is ready to play basketball. We will probably have to start the season without him, but hopefully he will be in the lineup quickly. Ah! Here comes the food let's eat!"

After everyone was served, Marv asked, "Thomas, would you ask the Lord to bless our food?"

"Certainly", Thomas answered.

"LORD, we thank you for the opportunity to have been in your house today. Now we ask for your blessing upon this food that we are about to partake. Thank you for this time together. We pray in JESUS name. AMEN."

After the meal and more conversation, the group headed home. Marv dropped off Ralph, then the Chaimberbrook family and went on home. It was a good day! Everyone seemed to enjoy themselves. Even Ralph was in a spirited mood! He thanked Marv and Thomas again and again for asking him to join them in church. "I really enjoyed it very much", Ralph said. "It felt good to be back in church again."

8

The days and weeks passed by; the football team kept on struggling. Without star receiver Nathan Boone in the lineup, the team was forced to play more of a ground game. Senior fullback Jeff Larkin did the bulk of the bull work, averaging over 100 yards per game. But even with that kind of effort, the team scored infrequently. The defense was overworked, and each game became harder and harder. After seven games their record stood at 0-7 with one game left to try and salvage the season.

Meanwhile, fan support for the team was, unfortunately, slacking off. People were focusing more on the World Series, another 'Fall Classic' that featured the New York Yankees and the Los Angeles Dodgers. The Yankees entered the series with the best record in baseball, at 104-57, 10 ½ games ahead of the Chicago White Sox. They were also two-time defending World Champions. But that did not intimidate the Dodgers, as Los Angeles swept the series 4-0, allowing the mighty Yankees only four runs for the entire series!

Sandy Koufax beat Whitey Ford twice to win the MVP award. Don Drysdale and Johnny Padres along with ace reliever Ron Perranoski finished off the Yanks in the other games. It was the first time the Yankees had been swept in a four game series.

Then came the last Saturday in October, a modest crowd was settling in for the team's last football game of the season........

"Sure would be nice if we could win at least one game this year", Marv was talking to Thomas as they sat together in the stands. "Ryan High only has one win so far this season, so maybe we can pull one out of the bag here."

"Yeah, maybe", Thomas answered. "It sure would help if we had a few more fans here to cheer the team on."

"Well, it's only 40 degrees, so that isn't helping draw the fans either. So where is the rest of the family today?"

"Tom is over at Larry's playing some one-on-one, and Martha is home with an earache. She stayed out in that cold wind a little too long yesterday, so she decided to stay home."

"Yeah, Sandy decided to stay home as well. It is chilly out here today especially with that breeze blowing. Well. It looks like they are about ready to kickoff."

Ryan High kicked off and sophomore speedster Loren Drake took the ball at the Limestone 12 yard line. Running straight up field, he evaded two tacklers and quickly cut to the left sideline.

Swiftly moving along the sideline he raced all the way to the Ryan 20 yard line before changing directions, cutting back to the center of the field, avoiding the last two tacklers, and cruising into the end zone for an 88 yard TD run!

The fans went ballistic! It was Limestone's first kickoff return for a touchdown in over two years!

"Wow, did you see the speed of that kid?" Marv asked excitingly. "Where has he been hiding all this time?"

"Just brought him up from the JV team this week", a man in front of them stated. "Kid has blistering speed, should have called him up before now."

"Wow", Marv stated. "That sure was exhilarating to watch! I wonder if the kid can play basketball?" he asked to no one in particular.

"We will have to wait and see if he comes out for the team next week", Thomas spoke up. "Sure could use some of that speed on the court."

The Limestone defense stopped Ryan on three plays after the ensuing kickoff and took over on their own 49 yard line after a poor punt.

Rick Jackson hit Drake for a 32 yard gain on the first play from scrimmage, moving the ball to the Ryan 19. Handing the ball off to his fullback on the next play, Jeff Larkin blasted up the middle to the 3 yard line.

On first and goal from the 3, Jackson took it in himself, untouched. With just a little over a minute gone in the game, Limestone had taken a commanding 14-0 lead!

The cold weather didn't matter much anymore at this point. The hometown crowd was being treated to something they had not seen all season. The onslaught continued, as Ryan never got into the game. Limestone blasted Ryan 48-0!

The fans stormed the field after the game, carrying off Coach Norman Yandowski on their shoulders. You would have thought they just won the State Championship! Celebrations lasted until well into the evening.

"What a way to finish!" Marv stated excitingly as he jumped up and down. "Let's hope that excitement can carry over into the basketball season."

"Yeah, that sure was exciting", Thomas came back. "Best high school football game I believe I have ever seen. Of course, I may be a little partial to the home team."

"It's only the beginning, Thomas! Catch the fever! We are in for an incredible ride! My bones feel it! This will be the season that this town won't forget for a long time!"

"I hope you are right my friend", Thomas came back.

"I am!" Marv declared. "You watch, we are going to make it happen!"

The day finally arrived......November 1st, first day of practice.......

Eighteen kids showed up for opening day practice, including the injured Nathan Boone, still walking on crutches. Marv was a little disappointed, he was hoping for a larger turnout. "Alright you guys, have a seat." Marv began.

'First of all I want to introduce my new assistant this year. This is Coach Thomas Chaimberbrook, he will be helping me form this team into what I believe is going to be a pretty good ball club"

Several of the players turned their heads towards Tom. "Yes, that's right", Marv said. This is Tom's Dad. We are fortunate to have Tom with us this year; I believe he will be a tremendous asset to our team.

'I see we have some new faces that have come out; I want to welcome all of you. Everyone will get an opportunity to make the team; however, we will only be carrying 12 on the roster to begin the season. Don't be disappointed if you don't make the cut. If you play well on the JV team there is always a possibility you will be called up to the varsity.

'Alright now get out there and get warmed up. We will play a little scrimmage after a while."

Marv emptied the ball rack onto the floor as all the players grabbed a ball and began shooting baskets.

"Thomas, come on over here. Let's talk for a minute", Marv said.

The two sat down on the bench, and Marv pulled out a sheet of paper. "Here is the list of who we have signed up so far. Now I am going to start out by working with the seniors and juniors on one end of the court, and I want you to work with the sophomores and freshmen on the other end.

'Just watch them shoot for a while and kind of get a feel who you might think could fit with the team. We will get into it deeper as we go along. This is the first day, so we are more or less just taking a look at what we have got."

"Alright I'll see what I can do", Thomas said.

"Okay, Gentlemen", Marv hollered out. "All seniors and juniors come with me, sophomores and freshmen go with Coach Chaimberbrook down to the other end."

The two squads split up. Marv put the seasoned team through some drills. He wanted to get Tom into the mix of some of their plays.

The focus was, always look for the open man. But now that Tom was in the middle to take care of any rebounds, it left the shooters an option to gamble a little more on their shot selection.

And with Tom's tremendous skills under the basket, the opportunity to open up the offense was obvious to Marv. He stood in awe watching as his veterans went through their drills.

Meanwhile, Thomas watched the younger kids at the other end. He was impressed by sophomores Vidal Holbrook and Jose Demarez and a young freshman named Willy Stanfield.

Practice lasted until 5:30 that first evening. Marv called all of them aside at the end and said:

"Alright, good job all of you. I want to practice tomorrow morning at 10:00. We don't ordinarily practice on a Saturday, but with our first game just a week away, I feel like we need all the time we can cram in to prepare for that game. So all of you try to be here if you can; I'll see you then. Hit the showers!"

Turning to Thomas, he said, "Well what do you think?"

"I thought Holbrook, Demarez, and Stanfield looked pretty good. They all can shoot and Holbrook looks pretty strong on the boards."

"Good observation, Thomas. Holbrook and Damerez played some last year. Stanfield, I don't know much about him. He was a new kid last year, and played a little on the JV squad, but we will take a good look at him and see what he can do."

"How did it look from your end?" Thomas asked.

"Fantastic! Your son has incredible skills, Thomas. With the right chemistry, there is no telling how far this team can go."

"Well, I guess we will see just how good we are when we play Adirondack Parochial next Friday night. I understand they are a very good team."

"That is an understatement! They have won the Northern Regional for the past two years. We played them last year in our first game also. They ripped us good, 79-58 if I recall correctly. That game was on their court, so playing at home this time should make a difference."

"Let's hope so. See you in the morning."

Saturday morning practice went smoothly. Only 14 showed up, but all the returning players were there, as well as Tom, of course.

Ralph Stevens stopped by to catch a glimpse of the action. After practice he approached Marv and Thomas……..

"The team looks pretty good." Ralph stated. "You guys are doing a great job getting them ready. I am looking forward to the first game."

"Believe me Ralph", Marv answered, "So are we. Now when you get here Friday night, you come right over to the bench. I will have a seat for you right behind us, alright?"

"Well, thank you Marv, I really appreciate that. See you guys in church tomorrow!"

"Whoa! Did you hear that?" Thomas said as Ralph left. "He said he would see us in church tomorrow! I see a new skip in Ralph's step. Did you notice, Marv?"

"Sure did. It is great to see him coming out of his doldrums. You have really given him some much needed encouragement, Thomas."

"Not me, Marv. It's the LORD working with him. There is a new spark in his eyes; Praise God!"

9

Monday afternoon at 4:00 practice………

"Alright guys", Marv was hollering out, "Get warmed up. Today we are going to really get at it; an all-out scrimmage. I want you guys to play like you were in a real game. So get loosened up, then we will start."

"Sorry I am a little late coach", Nathan Boone shouted as he came hobbling in the gymnasium, without crutches!

"Wow!" Marv shouted with excitement. "When did you get that cast off your foot?"

"I just got it off this morning." Nathan answered. "Doctor said it would probably be a couple of more weeks before I can play, but he said I could start working out with the team as long as I took it easy."

"That's great news, Nate. Yeah, go ahead and warmup a little with the guys, but don't overdo it!"

"Thanks, Coach. And don't worry, I won't get too rambunctious out there; I want to play as soon as I am able."

"And we want you to play as soon as possible as well."

Marv called Thomas over to the side and said; "Alright, Buddy. Now is your first shot at coaching. You are going to coach one side and I will coach the other."

"This sounds like a setup to me", Thomas answered smiling. "You get all the good players and I get what is left over!"

"That's right", Marv agreed. "I am taking Tom, Larry Jones, Steve Woods, Rick Jackson, and Vidal Holbrook, and you have got the rest."

"Gee, Thanks Ole Buddy."

"Ha! Ha! Ha!" Marv laughed. "Don't worry; we are going to mix it up after a while. I want to take a look at what will probably be our starters for a bit, and then we will switch around. Besides, I also want to take a look at YOU! I know you can coach, Thomas; so show me what you can do!"

"Alright, wise-guy; I'll show you."

Marv called the players together, and took the five he picked to the other side of the court, leaving Thomas scratching his head.

"Alright, gang", Thomas began. "Let's show them rag-tags over there what we can do. Fred (Long), you get in the middle. Let's try Demarez and Stanfield at the guards, and Lucas (Nick) and Baker (Stu) at the forwards. Go get'em."

Marv tossed the ball up, and they were off. After about a fifteen minute deluge off continuous lopsidedness, Marv mercifully stopped the action. "Alright fellas", Marv said. "Great job; now let's mix it up a little. Tom and Rick go over to the other side, and Jose and Willie come on over here. Alright, let's roll."

The change made a big difference in the competition. With Tom and Rick working with the younger players, the sides were much more even. They worked at different plays and defenses for the rest of the practice. At the end, Marv was well pleased.

"Great job you guys. We are really getting into the groove now. Hit the showers! See you tomorrow at 4:00."

Walking off the court Marv turned to Thomas, "Not bad for your debut, Thomas. See, I told you it would come natural. You are going to be a great coach."

"I have got a long ways to go to catch up with you, Marv. You have about seven years' experience on me."

"You will catch on fast, Thomas. Just go with the flow. You have a good eye for talent. You're right about that Stanfield kid. He can shoot, and he has quick hands.

'And I like what you did putting Long in the pivot. He played a little last year at forward, but I have never tried him at center. That may be an option we can look at if we need too. But with Tom in there, we probably won't need to go that route."

"You never know, Marv. It's always good to have a backup plan if needed."

"See, you are starting to think like a coach already! It is getting into your blood now isn't it? Come on now admit it!"

"Ha! Ha! Ole Marv, you never can get basketball off your mind. Come on, you 'Old Rascal' you; let's go grab a burger, what do you say?"

"Have I ever turned down food? Let's go!"

Tuesday afternoon at practice.........

The team was warming up and Marv and Thomas were planning their strategy for the day's practice, when a small kid around 5 feet 6 inches walked in the gym and skittishly asked Marv; "Ah, Coach is it too late to try out for the team?"

Marv looked up at the lad and replied; "Well, hello there Partner. What is your name?"

"Loren Drake, Sir."

Marv looked at Thomas, and Thomas looked back at Marv, and both of them had a big smile on their faces.

"Sorry, Loren", Marv replied. "I didn't recognize you without your football uniform on. I watched you play last Saturday; I was very impressed with what I saw."

"Thank you, Sir."

"To answer your question, no, it is not too late to try out. Ever played much basketball, Loren?"

"No, Sir, and I realize I am petty small, but I would like to give it a shot if you are willing to take a chance on me?"

"Well, I will tell you what, I have seen you run. Speed on a basketball court can sometimes be very advantageous. You got any gym shorts you can change into real quick?"

"Yes, Sir, I have some shorts in my gym locker."

"Go get them on and get back up here. We will give you a shot."

"Thank you, Sir", Loren said as he turned and headed for his locker.

"Can you believe this?" Marv said turning to Thomas. "We were wondering if he could play basketball; guess we are about to find out."

"Yup", Thomas answered. "He sure is a lot smaller than he looked in a football uniform."

"Yeah, but if he can dribble the ball, we may be able to use him at guard. Just think what he might be able to do on a fast break. I tell you, Thomas, there may be some potential in that little guy."

A couple of minutes later, Loren was back on the floor in his shorts and tee shirt. "Okay, Loren", Marv began. "You go on down there to the other end of the court and work out with Coach Chaimberbrook and that bunch down there."

"Yes, Sir." Loren ran off down to the other end.

Marv continued to drill his seniors and juniors while Thomas was putting the younger players through some plays. He pulled Loren off to the side and had him taking shots at a side court basket.

"Just shoot away, Loren", Thomas said. "After you get loosened up a bit, I'll put you in the mix of some of our drills."

After a few minutes, Thomas called his players over, and started putting them through some dribbling exercises. He was particularly watching Loren Drake to get a feel on how well, he could handle the basketball. Thomas was impressed; Loren did surprisingly well.

Marv blew his whistle and gathered everyone around. "Alright, guys, time to get down to business. We have two more practices after today before our first game. Tomorrow I will be making the cut, so if you have been holding anything back, now is the time to show it.

'We are going to do some serious scrimmaging, and I want you to play as if you were in an actual game. Rick and Tom will choose up sides, and then we will go at it. I am going to flip a coin; Tom you call it."

Marv flip the coin in the air. "Heads", Tom called. It landed 'tails'.

"Rick, you choose first." Marv said.

The two selected their choices; Marv took Tom's team and Thomas took Rick's. Marv tossed the ball up at center court, and the two squads went at it. Both teams played hard for about ten minutes, took a short one minute time out, made some substitutions, and went at it again.

This went on for a good hour before Marv finally stopped the action. By this time everyone was panting and puffing, sweat pouring off everybody, including Marv and Thomas.

"Alright, gang, that's it for tonight. Everybody did great. That was an awesome workout. See you tomorrow at four o'clock. Hit the showers!"

As Marv and Thomas were gathering up the equipment, Marv turned to Thomas and said, "What do you think, Thomas. Are we getting anywhere with these kids?"

"I think they are shaping up just fine, Marv. That Drake kid has potential. I am sure you seen how he handled that fast break that Jackson threw to him?"

"Sure did, looked like he was throwing him a long pass on the football field. Man can that kid fly!"

"Think he is good enough for varsity play?"

"I don't know yet. He is a little rough on the edges, but we can mold him into a good player I believe. We will take a good look at everybody tomorrow before we determine who will make the cut.

'Of course we will have to make room for Nathan Boone when he is well enough to play. So that will give us an extra player to start out with. We will see."

After Wednesday's practice Marv told the players that the final selection would be on the sports bulletin board in the morning. Thursday morning all the players checked the sports bulletin board first thing.

Final Cut
The following players report for practice this
evening at 6:15.
Tom Chaimberbrook
Rick Jackson
Larry Jones
Steve Woods
Fred Long
Vidal Holbrook
Jose Demarez
Willie Stanfield
Nick Lucas
Leon Brown
Stu Baker
Montgomery Alexander
Nathan Boone
All other players report to JV coach George
Farmington at 4:00.   Coach Marvin Smith

Thursday evening………

Marv arrived at the gymnasium at 5:30. He
wanted to watch the younger players working out
with Coach Farmington. He was keeping a particular
close-eye on Loren Drake. But there was also
another kid out there that caught his eye.

The kid showed some outstanding shooting ability and could handle the ball very well. When the practice ended around 6:00, Marv walked over to Coach Farmington and asked, "George who is that young kid right there just going out the door?" He said pointing.

"Oh, that would be Tommy Jones", George answered. "Looks pretty good, doesn't he?"

"He sure does. I don't believe I've seen him around here before. Is he a new kid this year?"

"New as a freshman, yes. He came in from Limestone Junior High School this fall. You have his brother on the varsity!"

"What? You mean to tell me that is Larry Jones' brother?"

"Yup, that's right. Great kid too, I guess it runs in the family."

"Obviously; Keep an eye on him George, and on Loren Drake as well. Let me know if you feel they are ready for varsity play."

"Will do, Marv; I'm looking forward to tomorrow night should be a great game."

"I hope we can give them a game this year, George. We got trounced last year."

A few minutes later, Thomas brought the varsity squad into the gym. Marv emptied the ball rack, and the players started warming up.

"I've been watching a little of the JV practice", Marv spoke to Thomas. "That Drake kid is going to be okay I believe in a few weeks. I also saw another young kid that looked pretty good. His name is Tommy Jones; name sound familiar?"

"Pretty common name, I'd say", Thomas replied. "Sort of like Smith."

"Common, yes; it happens to be Larry Jones' brother."

"Yeah, Tom told me that Larry had a younger brother, but I've never met him."

"Nor have I. But I hope to get to know him soon."

Marv put the team through a very vigorous workout for two plus hours. At the end, everyone was panting and sweating like crazy. He called the team over to the bleachers.

"Alright, everybody, have a seat. I don't have to tell you how good our opponent is tomorrow night. Most of you are aware of what they have done for the last two or three years. Coach Phil Phillips has done a marvelous job with that team; I see no reason to believe they will be anything less this year. I believe that we have got a shot at them this time around. It is going to take a tremendous team effort to beat them, but we can do it! Do you guys believe that?"

Everyone agreed they could win. "You bet Coach, we can take them down."

"Good, that's the attitude I want to hear. Be at the dressing room by 6:00 tomorrow night. Game time is 7:00. One more thing, starting next week we will be practicing at 6:15. The JV's will practice at 4:00. Anybody got any questions?" no reply. "Alright, hit the showers."

10

Friday evening……..

A large crowd started pouring into the Limestone gymnasium shortly after they opened the doors at 6:00. The Watertown radio station WATR was on hand to cover the game. Several fans had their portable radios tuned into the game as it came on the air at 6:30.

"Good evening ladies and gentlemen. WATR welcomes you to our first basketball broadcast of the season. Tonight's game features the two-time defending Northern Regional Champion Adirondack Parochial Monarchs verses the Limestone High Raiders. I'm Paul Paulson your play-by-play announcer for tonight's game, along with Jim Jacobs who will be bringing you his color analysis and commentary. Well, Jim it looks like we have quite a crowd gathering here for tonight's game!"

"Yes, Paul, and this could be quite a contest tonight. Limestone High has a senior newcomer in the lineup this year that already has built up quite a reputation. Tom Chaimberbrook transferred here from Mount Carmel High School in Indiana where he led that team to their first ever conference championship last year. At 6 foot 8 inches, he is an outstanding force on the inside.

'Adirondack's 6 foot 7 inch center, Jeffery Davidson, will have his hands full tonight trying to contain Chaimberbrook. It should be a great match up."

"Alright, Jim, I see the teams are coming out on the floor now for their warmups. We will be right back with tonight's starting lineup."

As the station broke for a commercial, Marv got the wives and Ralph Stevens seated right behind the bench. "Great seats Marv, thank you", Ralph said.

"No problem, enjoy the game", Marv responded.

He then went out to center court to talk with Adirondack's coach Phil Phillips. "Good evening, Phil", Marv said holding out his hand.

"Hello, Marvin, good to see you again", Phil answered back shaking Marv's hand. "You have a new kid out there I see. Don't remember him from last year?"

"That's Tom Chaimberbrook, new transfer from Indiana."

"Ah, yes, I've heard of him. Good player I understand."

"Best player I've ever had the privilege to coach. We should give you some competition tonight."

"Great, I'm looking forward to it. My team needs a good challenge. It keeps them on their toes."

Just then the radio announcer came back on the air. "Well, the teams are getting about ready to go, so here is tonight's starting lineup. First for Adirondack Parochial……At the guards will be 6 foot senior Ronnie Johnson and 5 feet 11 inch junior Jeremy Phillips. At center is 6 foot 7 inch senior Jeffery Davidson. At the forwards, 6 feet 6 inch senior Michael Sweeny and 6 feet 5 inch junior Chad Shumway. The head coach for Adirondack Parochial is Phil Phillips.

'Now for Limestone High……Starting at the guard positions, 6 foot 2 inch senior Larry Jones and 6 foot junior Rick Jackson. At center is 6 feet 8 inch senior Tom Chaimberbrook. And at the forwards, 6 foot 5 inch senior Steve Woods and 6 foot 7 inch sophomore Vidal Holbrook. The head coach for Limestone High is Marvin Smith.

'We are just seconds away from the opening tip in what should be an interesting game tonight, Jim"

"That's right Paul. And the fans are still pouring in, looks like we are going to have a full house and then some. It has been awhile since Limestone has seen this big of a crowd; it could be a record breaker tonight."

"Alright, here we go! The ball is up, and Chaimberbrook controls the tip over to Jones who quickly brings the ball down the right side line. He looks inside; Chaimberbrook is covered up by Davidson. He passes over to Jackson, down the left side to Woods. He shoots from 20 feet. Off the rim, no good; rebound Davidson.

'He throws out to Phillips on the left side; down court quickly to Johnson. He drives the lane and lays it up and in! Adirondack is on the board first.

'Jones inbounds to Jackson. He brings the ball down court looking for an open man. Stolen away by Phillips! He drives all the way down and lays it up and in!"

"Quick hands there by Phillips", Jacobs chimed in. "Bursting speed down court. Adirondack jumps out in front quickly."

"Jones inbounds again to Jackson. He brings the ball down; again being guarded closely by Phillips. Over to Jones; back out to Jackson; looking inside to Chaimberbrook, still double teamed. Into Woods; he shoots from 18 feet, no good; rebound Davidson.

'Long throw down court to Johnson; he drives the lane and shoots, good and he is fouled by Jones! Free throw is good; 7-0 Adirondack.

'Jones inbounds; intercepted by Phillips; over to Sweeny, he drives and scores and is fouled by Holbrook! Free throw is good; time out Limestone! Coach Smith is not a happy camper over there on the sidelines, Jim"!

"Not happy at all, Paul. Wow, Adirondack looking like the force they have been for the past couple of years. They have come out of the gate swinging and have taken a commanding 10-0 lead early in this game."

"Well let's see if that time out has helped Limestone get on track. I see a substitution; Fred Long, a sophomore, now is in for Steve Woods.

'Long inbounds to Jackson, who quickly brings the ball up court and into the middle to Chaimberbrook who fakes left, hooks right; good! Limestone is finally on the board!

'Phillips inbounds to Johnson; he throws down court to Sweeny who pulls up and shoots. Blocked by Chaimberbrook! Out to Jones; up court to Jackson; he shoots from 25 feet; yes! And he is fouled by Phillips! Free throw is good. And the Raiders are right back in it!"

"And so is the crowd, Paul", Jacobs interjected. "Listen to that roar as they see their team coming back against that early onslaught by the Monarchs."

"Phillips again on the inbound pass to Johnson. He works his way down court; throws over to Shumway; deflected by Holbrook! Out to Jones; quick throw down court to Jackson, driving the lane, up and in! And he is fouled again by Phillips! Free throw good; time out Adirondack!"

"Now it is Coach Phillips that is upset, Paul", Jacobs jumped in. "He obviously didn't like that last foul call on his son Jeremy. He is over there arguing with referee Al Turner over that call. He had better be careful, Paul. Yep, there it is the big T!"

"Technical foul, on Adirondack coach Phillips. Let's see who will shoot the free throw. It looks like Rick Jackson. Yes and the free throw is good! Phillips now out of the lineup and is being replaced by sophomore Arthur Lane.

'Limestone will retain possession under their own basket. Jackson into Long; he shoots from 20 feet; off the rim no good. Rebound Holbrook; he slams it home! Limestone takes the lead!"

"Wow, what a comeback!" Jacobs blurted out excitingly. "Down by 10 early; now right back in it. This crowd is going berserk!"

The two teams exchanged baskets through the remainder of the first quarter which ended 19-18, Limestone.

"As we start the second quarter, Steve Woods is back in for Limestone, and Jeremy Phillips, with two fouls on him, is back in for Adirondack.

"The ball is up and again Chaimberbrook controls the tip over to Jones. He passes off to Jackson; inside quickly to Chaimberbrook; he blows by Davidson and slams it down! The crowd is once again on their feet!

'Phillips into Johnson; he brings it down court; over to Sweeny; inside to Davidson. Davidson turns and shoots; blocked by Chaimberbrook! Out to Jackson; quickly up court to Woods; he shoots; off the rim. Rebound Chaimberbrook; Bang! He slams another one down!"

"Now we are starting to see why there is so much acclaim for Tom Chaimberbrook", Jacobs spoke up. "He has tremendous talent and is showing it off right now!"

Tom continued his rampage throughout the second quarter, and as the teams broke for halftime the scoreboard read Limestone 48, Adirondack 36!

In the Limestone locker room……..

"Alright guys, we have got them on the run", Marv began. "But we cannot let up. They are a well-disciplined team, and are quite capable of coming back on us.

'Great job in the middle, Tom; Rick, great shooting out there, and the ball movement is good. Vidal, great job on the boards. Just keep it up, all of you, with what you are doing; stay aggressive; hit the boards hard. Okay, let's go!"

In the Adirondack locker room.........

"What the hell are you guys doing out there?" Coach Phillips began. Are you going to let that big guy in the middle intimidate you all night? Jeffery, you have got to get on him. He is making you look silly. Michael and Chad, you have got to get in there and help out.

'We are better than this and you guys know it! Ronnie and Jeremy don't be afraid to take some outside shots. We have got to open up our offense. And everybody start hitting the boards hard! We can do this! We have done it before, we can do it again. Let's go!"

"Well we are about ready to start the second half, Jim Jacobs." Announcer Paul Paulson stated. "What do you make of this game so far?"

"Boy, we sure have seen a lot of excitement already, Paul. I expect more of the same in the second half. The key battle will be in the middle. Can Jeffery Davidson contain Tom Chaimberbrook? That is the big question as we get back underway."

"Alright, here we go. The ball is up and Chaimberbrook controls the tap over to Jackson; back across court to Jones; inside to Chaimberbrook. There is a big logjam in lane.

'Chaimberbrook cannot get loose and flips it back out to Jones. He shoots from 20 feet; off the rim and a huge collision under the boards as everybody is going for the rebound. Referee Al Turner calls for a jump ball! It is getting a little rough out there, Jim!"

"Yes, it looks like both coaches were telling their players to be aggressive on the boards. This could be quite interesting to watch."

"Chaimberbrook and Davidson will face off again near the Limestone end. The ball is up and Chaimberbrook controls, but it is intercepted by Phillips! Over to Johnson, who is quickly down court. Outlet pass to Sweeny; he shoots from 18 feet, yes! Here come the Monarchs, Jim."

"You can never count this team out, Paul! They have shown they can do this before, and it would not surprise me to see it happen again."

Adirondack continued to comeback. After three periods they had pulled to within two at 68-66. Rick Jackson and Larry Jones each picked up two fouls for Limestone. Jeremy Phillips picked up two more for Adirondack and was forced to sit starting the fourth quarter. Arthur Lane again replaced him.

"Alright, here we go with the fourth quarter. The ball is up and again Chaimberbrook controls. Jones takes the ball and drives hard down the lane crashing into Davidson! He is called for Charging! That will be three fouls on Jones!

'Lane feeds into Johnson who brings the ball up court. A quick pass to the inside! Davidson spins on Chaimberbrook and shoots; blocked by Chaimberbrook! Jackson picks it up; quick outlet pass to Jones. He drives inside and shoots; off the rim; rebound by the trailer Holbrook; Bang! He blasts it through the net!"

The crowd erupted and the sound was almost deafening. The battle forged ahead, back and forth. With three minutes left in the game, Jeremy Phillips fouled out. A minute later, Larry Jones fouled out for Limestone. Sophomore Jose Demarez replaced him. With one minute left the teams were tied at 86 all.

"Lane inbounds to Johnson. Johnson is bringing the ball up court slowly, looking for the open man and the last shot. He fires inside to Davidson; no room there. Back out to Johnson; over to Sweeny; he shoots from 18 feet; yes!

'30 seconds left. Demarez inbounds to Jackson; down court quickly; into Chaimberbrook. He fakes right and hooks left handed; over the top of Davidson and in! Time out Adirondack with 10 seconds left. We are tied at 88!"

"This game has lived up to everything that we expected", Jim Jacobs chipped in, trying hard to be heard over the roaring crowd. "It doesn't get much better than this, Paul. What a way to start off the season!"

"You got that right, Jim. This has been a great match-up; right down to the wire. Could we be looking at overtime? We shall see as the teams are back on the court.

'Shumway will feed the ball in under full court pressure by Limestone. He gets it into Johnson. He turns and flips to Lane; intercepted by Jackson! Quick throw to Demarez in the corner, He lets fly from 20 feet at the buzzer! YES!! Limestone wins it 90-88!!!"

11

Coach Phillips plunged his way over to the Limestone bench.

"Great game, Marvin", Phillips said shaking Smith's hand. You have a really good team there. That Chaimberbrook kid is terrific."

"Thank you, Phil. Yes he is a terrific player and a terrific kid as well. I expect you will be right there when the playoffs begin?"

"Well I hope so. This has been a very good test for us tonight. It tells me we have some work to do."

"I know you, Phil. You will adjust."

"Thanks, Marvin, and again congratulations!"

The two shook hands again and Phillips went back to his players who were still sitting on the bench in disbelief. The Limestone players and fans picked up Coach Smith and carried him off the court as the radio announcers were finishing up.

"All I can say is WOW!! What a game! Limestone High has upset Adirondack Parochial 90-88 in a barn-burner of a game that had to be fun to watch by everyone attending here tonight. What have you got for us, Jim?"

"I can't help but agree with all you have said, Paul. This has to be one of the greatest high school games I have ever seen. Now here are a few numbers for you stat junkies out there.

'Tom Chaimberbrook led all scorers with 37 points. He also had 12 rebounds and 7 blocked shots! Not a bad night I'd say. Rick Jackson tallied 20 and Larry Jones hit 18 before fouling out late in the game. But of course, the BIG basket was Jose Demarez' winning shot at the buzzer. He only scored those two points, but they were the biggest points of the night!

'Jeffery Davidson led Adirondack with 24 points, 10 rebounds, and 4 blocked shots. Michael Sweeny and Ronnie Johnson chipped in with 19 points each."

"Alright, thank you Jim. Well, that's it for our broadcast tonight folks. We hope you have enjoyed listening to the game. This is Paul Paulson along with Jim Jacobs saying goodnight from Limestone. Now back to our WART studios in Watertown."

Fans celebrated well into the night. After the gymnasium cleared out and the players were all in the shower room celebrating, Marv, Thomas, their wives and Ralph all went over to 'Hanks Diner' for a burger. The place was packed. Everyone was congratulating Marv and Thomas as they came in.

As they looked around for a seat, a man spoke up and said, "Here you go Coach, you can have this booth. We were just getting ready to leave anyway."

"Well thank you, Sir." Marv responded.

The wives slid into the booth first, then their husbands. Ralph pulled up an empty chair and sat at the end of the table.

"Haven't seen this much excitement in this town in a long time." Ralph spoke up with a big smile on his face.

"You see, Thomas", Marv said looking across the table to his friend and assistant. "Everybody is catching the fever! Just like I predicted they would. Fasten your seat belts everybody, we are in for a ride!"

Monday evening at 6:15 practice.......

Nathan Boone came slowly jogging into the gym and went right over to Coach Smith. "I think I'm about ready to play now, Coach", he announced.

"Whoa, hold on there, Partner. Let's not get ahead of ourselves. You look like you still have a slight limp there to me. Are you sure you are ready?"

"Yes Sir. Doc said when I felt I was able I could go for it."

"Well, we will see how things go in practice this week, Okay? I want you back in the lineup as well, but let's make sure you are ready. We will do some scrimmaging this week and see how it goes."

"Okay, Coach", Nathan said, grabbing a ball and trotting off to warm up.

"Well how about that, Thomas?" Marv said turning to his assistant. "We may be about to get even better."

Practice went well that week, with Marv keeping a close watch on Nathan Boone. At the end of Wednesday evening's practice, Marv decided that Nathan was about ready to play. To make room for him on the active roster, Montgomery Alexander was sent down to the JV's.

Thursday evening's practice was another hard work out to get the team ready for Friday night's game at Cedar Mountain Academy. At the end of practice Marv called the team over to the bleachers.

"Have a seat, Gentlemen", Marv began. "Great work tonight guys, you are all looking real good. Now tomorrow we will be playing our first road game. To be honest with you, I really don't know a whole lot about Cedar Mountain Academy. This will be the first time that we have ever played them, so we will just have to kind of play it by ear and see how things go.

'I was really impressed with the starting five we had in our first game, so we are going to go with the same starters again this week. I will try to get as many of you in the game as I can; depending of course on how the game goes.

'Everyone be here ready to board the bus at 6:00 PM. Remember the dress attire; shirt and ties, no exceptions! Understood? Any questions or comments?"

Freshman Willie Stanfield spoke up, "Coach, why is it we have to wear ties to away games, and the JV's don't?"

"Because you are VARSITY! You are representing Limestone High School! We want to show our opponents that we have a little class. This is why you wear ties. When the JV's make it to the varsity, the same rules will apply for them as well.

'Any other questions or comments? Aright, hit the showers! Nathan, I want to see you a minute."

After the rest of the team had left the gym, Marv said to Nathan, "I know you want to start, but I am still noticing just a slight limp in that injured foot. I will get you into the game as soon as I can, so be patient with me. I don't want to risk you reinjuring that ankle again."

"No problem, Coach, I understand. I'll be ready to play when you say so."

"Good attitude Nathan; I like that. Go get a shower!"

Friday evening……..

Excitement was in the air as the team boarded the bus and headed out for their first road game. The players were relaxed and joking with each other as they rolled along. Meanwhile, the coaches were planning their strategy for the night's game.

When they arrived at Cedar Mountain Academy, the JV team went straight to the locker room to get dressed for their game, while the varsity took their time looking over the new facilities before entering the gymnasium and getting seated for the first game.

With Limestone trailing by 10 as the third quarter ended, the varsity headed for the locker room to get dressed. When they returned, 15 minutes later, the JV game had just ended; Cedar Mountain 56, Limestone 47.

The varsity took to the floor as soon as it was cleared. Pregame drills went as usual. A few Limestone fans were on hand, including the coaches' wives, plus about thirty others.

Limestone got off to a tremendous start as Tom Chaimberbrook took control of the game immediately. As the guards kept feeding him the ball inside, Tom made some outstanding shots that had the crowd buzzing.

Building up a 20 point lead at halftime, Marv started Nathan Boone in the second half in place of Vidal Holbrook.

Boone got into the mix quickly, hitting his first three shots. Meanwhile Chaimberbrook continued his blistering pace, hitting from all directions and blocking shots at random.

With five minutes left, and the game well in control, Marv pulled Tom, Rick Jackson and Larry Jones. He moved Boone to center and brought Holbrook back into the game along with Willie Stanfield and Jose Demarez.

Before the game ended, everybody on the team got into the game! Limestone routed Cedar Mountain 98-65! Tom Chaimberbrook tallied his first triple double of the season; 49 points, 14 rebounds and 11 blocked shots!

Cedar Mountain coach Edward Perkins congratulated Marv after the game. "Good game Marvin", he began, shaking Marv's hand. "We were definitely out played tonight. That Chaimberbrook kid is fantastic! You guys should go a long way this year."

"Thank you Edward, I appreciate your comments. Yes, we are very fortunate to have Tom this year. He is an outstanding player; best one I've ever coached."

"I read about your win over Adirondack Parochial. That was quite an impressive victory; always a tough team!"

"Yeah, they trounced us good last year, so that was a really sweet win!"

"We play them next week. I was hoping that we could at least give them a game. But after tonight, I am not so sure."

"Well, good luck. They are a very good team as usual."

The two coaches shook hands once again and each headed for their respective locker rooms. A half hour later Limestone was on the bus headed back home. The players were pumped up after their big win and everybody was slapping Tom on the back and congratulating him on his magnificent performance.

Tom took it all in modestly, giving credit to all the players for feeding him the ball and helping out on the boards.

"Hey, you guys", Tom pointed out. "It was Vidal that led in rebounds, not me."

True, Holbrook grabbed 15 boards as opposed to Tom's 14. Boone added 8 more, playing only in the second half, plus scoring 12 points! A fact that Marv took into notice!

"I believe that Nathan Boone is about ready to start in our next game, Thomas. What do you think?"

"You are the boss, Marv. But if you are asking for my opinion, yes, I'd say he is ready. Not a bad showing tonight in only half a game."

"I agree. We will check things out in practice next week and if he still looks good without too much strain on that ankle, we will give him a shot."

Practice went well the following week. The players were really getting into the groove now. Marv and Thomas introduced some new plays and the team started working on them. Some of the plays were intended to get Nathan Boone more involved in the game.

Boone responded very well, and by the end of Thursday evenings practice, Marv had made up his mind to start him in Friday night's game against Grand Junction Academy.

Grand Junction was a school from the southern part of the state, in the Catskill Mountain region. Limestone had not played them since Marvin had been coaching. The two schools last played seven years prior. That game went into overtime, with Grand Junction winning by a point on a 'Hail Mary' last second shot.

This game had the potential of being another barn-burner and the town was all excited. A large crowd was expected, the players were psyched, and Marv and Thomas were pumped up.

Friday morning-------

Everyone was talking about the night's big game! One whole side of the gymnasium had been reserved for students in anticipation of a huge turnout.

WATR was going to be there once again to broadcast the event. The whole town was rocking!

However, Friday afternoon their world changed. Limestone, and indeed the entire nation, was about to be turned upside down!!!

12

Friday, November 22, 1963......1:45 PM EST.......

BUZZZZZ! The loud speaker sounded in every class room at Limestone High School. A stern and commanding voice came on over the intercom.

"This is Principle Haywood. All students, teachers and faculty, PLEASE give me your attention!

'We have just received word that the President of the United States, John F. Kennedy, has been shot in Dallas, Texas! We have no other details at this time; however, we are going to dismiss at two o'clock.   All students are to immediately report to their respective homerooms.

'Bus students; be ready to board your bus in 15 minutes. Students, who have their own transportation, may be excused as soon as they report to their homeroom teacher.

'ALL activities scheduled for this evening are hereby cancelled until further notice; this includes tonight's basketball game with Grand Junction Academy!

'We will reopen Monday morning at our regular time unless you are otherwise notified over the weekend. You are now immediately excused from your classes. Report to your homerooms! Be safe!"

Some students were happy to be dismissed from school early. Still others, like Tom Chaimberbrook, were totally perplexed as to what they had just heard.

Tom gathered up his books and reported to his homeroom. Having his own car, he was immediately dismissed.

When he arrived home he found his parents in the living room with their eyes glued to the television. All three of the major networks, ABC, NBC, and CBS, were carrying the shocking news!

As he entered the living room, Tom asked, "Dad, what does this mean? I don't understand. Why would anybody want to shoot the president of the United States?"

"Unfortunately, not everyone likes the way President Kennedy is governing", Thomas replied. "This is the way some deranged people react!"

"That's crazy, Dad. So how is the President, is he going to live or what?"

"I am afraid not, Son. He was pronounced dead by the Dallas coroner just a few moments ago. Vice-President Lyndon Johnson is taking the oath of office for the presidency aboard Air Force One as we speak."

"Do they know who did this, Dad?"

"They have a suspect in custody by the name of Lee Harvey Oswald! They believe he fired the shots that killed Kennedy, from the sixth floor of the Texas School Book Depository Building, as his motorcade passed by. Texas' governor Connally was shot also and is in a Dallas hospital in critical condition. Sadly, both of them were pretty much sitting ducks, riding in an open convertible."

The following day President Lyndon B. Johnson proclaimed that Monday November 25 would be a day of mourning for the American people. Television coverage continued almost non-stop as the events unfolded.

Sunday morning the Chaimberbrook family decided to stay home from church and stay tuned to what was going on in Dallas and Washington, DC. As they were watching on live television, the process of transferring Lee Harvey Oswald from the basement of the Dallas Police Headquarters to a more secure location to await trial, another shocking event took place!

Out of the crowd stepped a man with .38 caliber pistol and shot Oswald, as the nation watched in total disbelief!! The man was apprehended immediately and was later named as Jack Ruby, owner of several strip clubs in Dallas, who had ties with the Dallas mafia.

Sunday afternoon the Chaimberbrook family got a call from the high school principle stating that all of Limestone's schools would be closed Monday in honor of President Kennedy's burial. Schools would reopen on Tuesday morning at the regular time.

Later that evening the phone rang again. Martha answered it as her husband and son sat watching the still unbelievable events of the past 48 hours.

"Thomas, it is for you", Martha called out.

As Thomas made his way to the phone, he asked, "Who is it?"

"J. Edgar Hoover!" was Martha's reply.

With a curious look on his face, Thomas took the phone. "Hello, Mr. Hoover. What can I do for you?"

"Good evening, Thomas. I assume you are well aware of what has been going on the past couple of days?"

"Of course, Sir; I am sure the whole world is aware of it by now."

"The last time we talked, I told you I would keep you in mind if something came up. Well, something has come up! I need you here in Washington to help the bureau solve this case as quickly as possible. Be here tomorrow morning as soon as you can to be sworn in and…….."

"Wait just a minute!" Tom interrupted. "Are you asking me to just drop everything and jump on a plane and fly to Washington because you claim you need me to help solve the Kennedy assassination?"

"That is exactly what I'm asking you to do, Thomas; especially after what happened this morning with the shooting of Oswald. I suspect that there is a conspiracy of some kind going on and I……."

"No dice, Mr. Hoover", Thomas interrupted again. "I told you before, I don't believe I am the man you are looking for to do the kind of work you want done. I am sure you have plenty agents that are far better qualified than I am. So the answer is NO!"

"Chaimberbrook, what in HELL is wrong with you? This is the second time I have offered you a job with the FBI, that most people would jump at in a heartbeat, and you turn me down flat! I don't understand where you are coming from. You are certainly qualified to do this kind of work and I need you NOW!"

"First of all, I am NOT like most people, Sir. Secondly, I have already decided that I don't want to work for the bureau. And I……."

"Thomas", Hoover said, much calmer this time. "Remember what President Kennedy once said: *'Ask not what your country can do for you, ask what you can do for your country'*".

With that Thomas exploded. "With all due respect, Sir, I have served my country over the past 20 plus years! And I damned near got myself killed on several occasions doing it! So I don't need a lecture from you, or anyone else, about 'What can I do for my country'. Do I make myself clear?"

Silence on the other end of the line for several seconds.

"Sir, are you still there?" Thomas asked.

"Yes, Thomas, I'm still here." Hoover came back, in a much milder tone this time. "And you are absolutely right. You have served your country, and quite admirably I might add. Quite frankly, I am not used to people coming back at me the way you do. I respect that of you, Thomas. So I guess that any offer I may have in the future for you is now 'out the window'?"

"Yes Sir, it is", Thomas came back, calmer than before. "I appreciate you taking me into consideration for such a high profile position, but I am finished working for the 'government'. I hope you understand."

"I do now, Thomas. I won't be bothering you anymore; best of luck to you in the future."

"Thank you, Sir. Good night!"

With that Thomas hung up the phone, turned and saw Martha staring at him. "I guess you told Mr. Hoover where to go?" She said.

"In so many words, yes. I don't believe he will be calling here anymore. What's the latest?"

"They are finalizing plans for Kennedy's funeral tomorrow. It is going to be televised nationally, of course."

Monday schools and many businesses across the nation were closed. All across the nation American flags were flying at half- mast, and would remain so for the next 30 days.

Hundreds of thousands of people lined the Washington streets, and millions more were tuned in on their television sets, to watch the horse drawn caisson take President Kennedy's body to Arlington National Cemetery where he was buried with full military honors. His wife Jacqueline later lit an eternal flame to forever mark the gravesite.

The gripping news of the past four days events overshadowed the fact that Thanksgiving was just three days away!

Early Tuesday morning, Sandy telephoned Martha. "I know this is kind of a late notice", Sandy began. "But if you haven't made other plans, we would love to have you over for Thanksgiving dinner. Lori is coming in from Atlanta tomorrow and this would give you a chance to meet her."

"Wow, yes, I am so looking forward to meeting your daughter. With all that has been going on the last few days, we really hadn't made any plans for Thanksgiving. So yes, we appreciate the offer."

"Good. Come on over about 2:30 or three o'clock. We will eat around four. How does that sound?"

"That sounds great! We will see you then."

Tuesday evening at practice…….

As the players were finishing up the warmups, Marv called everyone to the bleachers. "Have a seat", he began. "I received word this afternoon that our Thanksgiving tournament in Watertown this weekend has been canceled out of respect as to what has happened over the weekend. This means that we will not be playing again until a week from Friday night, December 6 to be exact.

'So with that in mind, we are going to just have a short light workout tonight and we won't be practicing at all tomorrow night. This will give you guys a few days off to spend time with you families over the Thanksgiving holiday. We will get back to work next Monday when we come back.

'In the meantime, if you guys want to stay in shape, you are certainly welcome to work out on you own. In fact, I would encourage you to do so. Okay, let's run a few plays, and we will get out of here early."

Marv worked the team lightly for about an hour and dismissed them. Heading back to Marv's office, he asked Thomas, "Well I guess you guys are coming over for Thanksgiving?"

"Yes, Martha told me that Sandy had called this morning. We appreciate the invite. We really hadn't planned anything; I guess it kind of slipped up on us after all the excitement over the weekend. So I understand your daughter is coming in for a few days?"

"Yeah she is. We are going down to Syracuse tomorrow afternoon to pick her up at the airport. It will be the first time she has been home since she left for college last August."

"Well I know you will be excited about seeing her. Three months is a long time not to see your daughter."

"Yes it is, but it is also a sign of her maturity. She is only 18 but you might think she is 25 the way she thinks. She is a very smart young lady."

"I am sure she is. And again, we do appreciate the invite. You be careful driving to Syracuse tomorrow. We will see you Thursday afternoon then."

"Great! See you then."

13

Thanksgiving Day..........

The Chaimberbrook family arrived at the Smith's at 2:45 that afternoon. They were greeted at the door by Marv.

"Well Happy Thanksgiving folks, come on in. Got the football game on TV and Sandy is busy in the kitchen!"

"Something sure does smell good", Thomas said.

Just then Sandy came around the kitchen corner and said, "Hi everybody. Martha you can give me a hand in the kitchen if you want. We will let the men watch football and chat. Sorry gentlemen, it is still going to be awhile before we eat."

"I will be glad to help you out Sandy", Martha spoke up. "So where is Lori? I can't wait to meet her."

"Oh she is upstairs getting changed. She will be down in a minute. So good to have her home; it has been three months since we have seen her."

Five minutes later, Lori came down stairs.

"Ah, there she is", Sandy spoke up. "Martha and Thomas, this is our daughter Lori!"

"So pleased to meet you Lori", Martha said, up as she gave Lori a hug."

"Lori, it is indeed a pleasure", Thomas replied.

"Pleased to meet you both", Lori replied. "Mom has been filling me in a lot about you folks."

"And, Lori, this is their son Tom", Sandy said turning to Tom who seemed engrossed in the football game.

As Tom arose to greet Lori, he stood speechless staring at her. Lori, on the other hand, was doing the same thing. Neither said anything!

"Ah, Lori, Tom, do you two know each other?" Marv inquired.

Snapping out of his trance, Tom simply said, "I, ah, I am pleased to meet you Lori."

"Oh, ah, yes, pleased to meet you too, Tom", Lori shyly answered.

Thomas looked at Martha, who had a big smile on her face, as if to say, 'I told you so'.

"Lori", Sandy spoke up. "You don't need to help me anymore in the kitchen. Why don't you and Tom take a little walk down by the river? It is still going to be almost an hour or so before we eat".

"Ah, sure, okay; want to go for a walk Tom?"

"Sure, I am not all that interested in the game anyways."

The Smith's lived just a short walk away from the Limestone River. As Tom and Lori slowly meandered along Tom spoke up first.

"So how is college going? Must be quite an adjustment from high school?"

"Well the studies are much harder, of course, but I am enjoying it. It is quite a change being away from home and all, but I have several friends there and they keep me company."

"So what are you studying?"

"Computer science is my major. I believe computers are the up and coming technology, and I am hoping to get in on the ground floor."

"Sounds interesting; who knows, someday they may have computers in the classrooms all across America."

"I believe that will happen, and it may be sooner than we think. But in case it doesn't, I am also taking a business course for a backup. There are always jobs for secretaries and receptionists.

'So what about you, Tom? What happens after high school? College basketball I assume? I understand you are a pretty good player?"

"Well, I don't know about that. I like to play basketball and may play in college, but I want to study something that I can make a career out of. I don't think professional basketball is in my future."

"That sounds very mature to me. Most boys our age, all they think about is sports. Same is true in college. It is either sports, or partying."

"So, speak about boys our age, I suppose you have a beau at college?"

"Not a chance! Bunch of immature adolescence in my opinion! Besides, I am there to study. No time for boys!"

"I see. Well, I guess that would rule out a date while you are home for a few days?"

"What?" Lori was somewhat shaken by Tom's question. "Are you asking me for a date?"

"In a roundabout way, yes, I guess I am. Forgive me for obviously being so bold. I didn't mean to offend you."

"Ah, no, I am not offended. I am just a little surprised that's all. And yes, I would like to go out with you."

"You would? I mean like wow! I never would have expected you to say yes."

"Well, for right now though, we had better get back to the house. Mom has probably got everything about ready by now."

"Yeah, come to think of it, I am a little hungry."

The two of them arrived back at the house just as Sandy and Martha were putting the food on the table.

"Perfect timing you two", Sandy said. "We are about ready to eat."

"Alright guys", Sandy called out. "Tear yourselves away from that television; time to chow down."

After everyone was seated, Marv asked the blessing.

"Dear Lord: We thank you for the opportunity to give you thanks today for all that you do for us. You are so merciful and long suffering, and yet always willing to forgive us for our sins. Thank you Father, and now may we have your blessing upon this food. May we partake of it as nourishment for our bodies and for our souls. It is in the precious name of Jesus that we pray. Amen!

'Alright everybody, dig in."

The two families enjoyed a full Thanksgiving feast: Roast Turkey, Stuffing, Mashed Potatoes and gravy, Yams, Green Beans, Carrots, Rutabaga, Gelatin Salad, Cranberry Sauce, Rolls and butter. All of this topped off with Pumpkin Pie, Apple Pie and Ice Cream!

After the meal, the women cleaned up in the kitchen while the men went back to watching more football. Later, Tom and Lori went out on the back porch and did a little star gazing before the Chaimberbrook's left for home. Tom made arrangements with Lori for a date Saturday night.

"I'll pick you up about six o'clock. We can grab a bite to eat and maybe take in a movie. How does that sound?"

"Sounds great to me, Tom; I haven't been to a movie in quite a while. Anything playing now that is worth watching?"

"The new James Bond flick is playing at the Pioneer Drive-In. I've heard it is supposed to be a blockbuster."

"Yeah, so I've heard. We will just play it by ear. I'll see you Saturday night."

"I'm looking forward to it. See you then."

Saturday evening……..

Being on time was Tom's main objective. He pulled into the Smith driveway at exactly six o'clock. Walking up to the front door, he was eagerly greeted by Lori.

"I will say this, Tom, you are punctual", she said.

"Or maybe a little too anxious", came Tom's reply. "I've been thinking about this since I left here Thursday night. So where would you like to go to eat?"

"Hank's Diner has good burgers and fries!"

"Alright, Hank's Diner it is."

Tom drove over to 'Hank's' where they both had a burger and fries and a milk shake.

"So how does James Bond sound to you tonight?" Tom inquired.

"I don't know, Tom; I am really not into this dating game thing much. How about we just go to the park and talk for a while, maybe get to know each other a little better?"

"I like that idea. I really would like to get to know you better, Lori. Besides, I'm not really into the 'Dating Game' either."

Tom drove over to the town park and parked. It was a beautiful moonlit night with the stars twinkling in dazzling display.

"Isn't the sky just beautiful tonight, Tom?"

"Absolutely magnificent; a brilliant display of God's incredible creation."

"It is so good to hear you talk like that, Tom. I don't know very many Christian boys at college. I guess that is why I am not too interested in dating any of them."

"But I am sure it is not because you have not been asked."

"Oh yeah, quite a few times; not interested."

"You are a beautiful girl, Lori; I am surprised someone hasn't gobbled you up by now."

"Thank you for the compliment, Tom, but I guess I am not ready for any commitment just yet."

"I understand, and frankly, neither am I. So when do you go back to Atlanta?"

"I fly back tomorrow afternoon; back in class Monday morning."

"Yeah, back to school Monday as well. I hope that maybe you can catch one of our basketball games sometime this season?"

"Well, I will be back in a couple of weeks or so. I get out December 18th for Christmas. Do you have any games scheduled during Christmas break?"

"Yes, I believe we have a couple."

"Great, I'll get to see you then. And with Dad being the coach, it won't cost me anything to get into the game."

"So do you like basketball?"

"Not particularly. But, of course, I have been exposed to it a lot with Dad being a coach and all."

"Of course; well I enjoy the game, but I have no aspiration of playing professionally. Too much travel involved and it makes it hard on a family if you are married.

'We moved around a lot when Dad was in the military. I was able to adjust rather easily, but it was tough on my Mom. She had almost the total responsibility of raising me."

"I would say she did a fine job. You are an extraordinary young man, Tom. I am so glad I met you."

"Believe me, the feeling is mutual, Lori. Frankly, there aren't very many girls that I pay much attention too. You, however, are an exception."

"Thank you for the flattery! Who knows, remarks like that MAY get you somewhere?"

"I was hoping it might", Tom said sheepishly.

"Yes, Well, I am glad we had this time to get a little better acquainted. But it's getting a little late, so maybe we better head back home."

"Sure thing", Tom came back, not wanting to blow his first date with the most beautiful girl he had ever seen!

He drove Lori back home and walked her to the door.

"I have enjoyed this evening, Tom. Really I have. And I will see you again in a couple of weeks."

"I will be anxiously awaiting that, Lori. You take care and I'll see you then."

With that, Lori reached up and gave Tom a quick kiss.

"Good night, Tom. Sweet dreams!"

"Good night, Lori. Be safe, it is a jungle out there! Don't get snared in a 'Wolf's trap'!"

Lori just smiled back and said softly. "Good night, Tom."

14

Sunday morning as the family was getting ready for church, Thomas asked Tom about the previous evening.

"Well how did your date with Lori go last night, Son?"

"I thought it went well for our first date. As it turns out, she isn't too much into the 'Dating Game' either so we just went over to 'Hank's' for a burger and then to the park and just talked. We were just kind of getting to know each other a little better."

"I see; so you didn't go to see a movie?"

"No, Lori said she wasn't into James Bond so we passed on that one."

"Well her Dad told me she was very mature for her age."

"Yes she is, and she is beautiful, Dad. I don't believe I have ever met a girl that can compare with her. So, ah, if we are about ready, I'll go start the car."

"Go ahead, Son. Your mother will be ready in a minute."

Just as Tom walked out the door, Martha came out of the bedroom.

"I overheard that conversation just now", she said with a big smile on her face. "I told you so, didn't I Thomas? My 'Woman's Intuition' was right on target!"

"Now Martha, don't go 'making a mountain out of a molehill', this was just a date for them to get acquainted."

"Ah huh; I told you they would be attracted to each other, which has become pretty obvious."

"And they don't need any prodding from you either", Thomas scolded.

"Thomas, I had nothing to do with this and you know it. They did this on their own, it was only natural."

"Okay, Martha. Let's just let things ride and see where it goes."

"Alright Thomas; 'We will see where it goes'", Martha sang as they walked to the car.

Sunday came and went. Monday it was back to business as usual. Practice went really well during the week as the team prepared for their upcoming away game at West Watertown High. The players were really anxious to get back on the court, and Tom seemed to have a little extra sprint in his step!

"The team looks really good, Thomas", Marv stated as they watched the players go through their final workout. "Tom seems like he is really on top of his game."

"Yeah, I have a feeling dating your daughter may have had something to do with that!"

"Uh huh; Lori did seem pretty relaxed around him. First sight attraction I guess."

"Well I hope it does not become a first sight 'distraction' for Tom, if you know what I mean?"

"I don't think so, Thomas. After all, Lori is away at college in Atlanta and Tom is here, so I don't believe they will be seeing a whole lot of each other any time soon."

"Well at least not for a couple of weeks or so", Thomas came back.

"What do you mean?"

"Well Tom told me she will be home for Christmas the middle of this month, so I reckon they will be seeing each other then?"

"Ah, Thomas, they are young. LIFE IS WHAT IT IS! Let them live it!"

"You sound like Ralph Stevens. I've heard him say that very same thing."

"Yeah, that's probably where I got it from. Look let's concentrate on the task at hand. We have a game tomorrow night. Keep your mind on the game!"

"Aye, Aye, Sir. I am a coach now. I've got to remember that."

"That's right, my friend. You are a coach now. Coaches have to stay focused."

Friday evening……….

The players were relaxed and talkative on the bus ride to Watertown. Spirits were high, the team had not played in three weeks, and they could not wait to get back on the court.

Once again Tom took immediate control of the game, banging in shots from every angle imaginable. On rare occasions when he was tied up in the middle, Rick Jackson and Larry Jones shot the lights out from the perimeter.

Limestone built up a 21 point lead at halftime. With seven minutes left in the game, and leading by 37 points, Marv pulled all the starters and put in the reserves. Everyone on the team played and scored.

Final score: Limestone 96, West Watertown High 69! Tom scored 42 points, Rick Jackson 21 and Larry Jones 18.

After everyone had showered and was accounted for, Marv had the bus driver stop at a local Baskins & Robbins and treated the entire team to ice cream cones.

"You guys earned it", Marv said with delight. "That was a great performance by everybody tonight. I'm proud of you guys."

The ride back home was a joyous one. Marv had the team singing songs, and then he would tell a joke or two that had everybody laughing.

Thomas, in the meantime, observed how Marv was able to interact with the players. *'This is what makes Marv such a great coach'*, he thought as he watched him. Not only did he have a natural basketball coaching ability, he had the respect of his players. Yup, coaching was definitely in his friend's blood!

Limestone moved on with a win over Green Mountain High in their next home game. The makeup game with Grand Junction Academy, meanwhile, had been rescheduled for Wednesday the 18th. Once again there was a capacity crowd on hand for what was expected to be a barnburner of a game. Both teams entered the game undefeated!

As the two teams were running their pregame warmup drills, Marv meandered out to center court to meet the new Grand Junction coach.

"Good evening Coach. I'm Marvin Smith."

"Good evening, Marvin. It's good to finally meet you in person. I'm Brian Niles."

The two men shook hands and Marv said, "So this is your first year at Grand Junction?"

"Yes, in fact it is my first year as head coach anywhere. I've coached some at the JV level and was assistant coach on the varsity for two years prior to this."

"Well looks like you are getting into the knack of it pretty quickly. I see you are 5-0 so far!"

"Yeah, we have gotten off to a pretty good start. You have also I see. By the way, that was an impressive win over Adirondack Parochial!"

"Well thank you. I've got a good team this year; hopefully we can have a good season."

"It doesn't hurt to have a Tom Chaimberbrook in the lineup", Niles came back quickly.

"Ah, so you know about Tom?" Marv asked.

"Not very many coaches around these parts that don't know about him, I'd say", was Niles' response. "Outstanding player can't wait to see him in action!"

BUZZZ! The buzzer sounded to clear the floor. As the teams were returning to their respective benches, Tom, as usual, looked up behind the bench where his mother sat. He came to an abrupt halt as he seen who was sitting between his mother and Sandy Smith. There was Lori!

As he approached the bench he said, "Whoa! What a pleasant surprise!"

"I told you I would be coming home for Christmas on the 18th. Here I am!"

"You didn't waste any time getting here."

"I knew you were playing tonight, so I made it a point to be here. I flew back this morning. Now show me what you can do!"

"I'll do my best", Tom smiled as he sat down.

A minute later, the game got underway; Tom controlling the tap to Larry Jones, but speedster Butch Higgins stole the ball from Jones and quickly drove the lane for a layup! Five seconds into the game and Grand Junction was on the board!

Nathan Boone inbounded to Rick Jackson who brought the ball down court. Jackson immediately went to the inside to Chaimberbrook. With a quick move Tom drove past the Grand Junction center and slammed it home! This brought the home town crowd to its feet!

And thus Tom went to work! With an explosive outburst, Limestone hit on nine straight shots, eight of them by Chaimberbrook!

Trailing 18-2 with just five minutes gone in the first quarter, Coach Niles had no choice but to call a timeout!

As the teams went to their benches, Tom looked up at Lori who was bubbling all over. Tom smiled back at her.

Tom was having an incredible night! With Limestone building up a 48-20 halftime lead, he already had 30 points at the half!

After three quarters, Grand Junction still trailed by 28 points. Marv pulled all of the starters except Tom.

"Why didn't you pull Tom also?" Thomas asked.

"He is having a tremendous night", Marv answered. "I want to see how the reserves play with him."

"I see", was Thomas' reply.

Marv put Fred Long and Steve Woods in at the forwards and Willie Stanfield and Jose Demarez at the guards, with Demarez running the point.

Grand Junction was able to close the gap slightly, but Tom continued his rampage. With five minutes left in the game Tom already had 61 points!

Refusing to score anymore himself, he kept passing the ball off so the others could score. Limestone crushed Grand Junction 98-73! Tom recorded a quadruple double for the night, 61 points, and 17 rebounds, dished out 10 assists, and blocked 11 shots!

Brian Niles congratulated Marv after the game. "That Chaimberbrook kid is absolutely fantastic!" he said excitedly.

"Yeah, he was sure on his game tonight!" Marv answered.

"Marvin you have done an outstanding job with that kid. You have got a superstar in the making. Boy that kid will go a long ways!"

"Thank you, Brian. But what you seen really did not have a whole lot to do with me. That is just raw talent out there!"

"Wow, I'll say! Anyways, good game Marvin, I'll see you again I hope."

"Good meeting you Brian. Take care."

A little while later…….

As Tom came out of the shower room and turned the corner heading for the exit door to the parking lot….there stood Lori, waiting for him!

"Wow, and what are you waiting for?" Tom asked coyly.

"Oh, I thought I might find someone here that would give me a ride home", Lori replied smiling.

"I see, well I guess I'll see you then." Tom smiled and walked out the door, leaving Lori standing there.

"Tom Chaimberbrook, where do you think you are going?" Lori demanded.

"Well I thought I would just go on home and do a little homework and go to bed. After all I have school tomorrow you know. And I guess you have someone that will give you a ride home?"

"You lug head, Tom! Who do you think I was waiting for?' Lori said disgustingly.

"Oh, I don't know", Tom said almost in a laugh. "Really Lori, I was just joking with you."

"Well, of course, if you don't want to take me home, I'll just call Dad and he will come and pick me up."

"Oh, I can see the headlines in the paper now.....STAR PLAYER THROWN OFF TEAM FOR REFUSAL TO TAKE COACH'S DAUGHTER HOME!"

"Ha! Ha! Ha! You really are funny, Tom".

"Come on Lori", Tom said walking back and putting his arm around her. "I guess I will take you home."

"I told Dad and Mom that I would wait for you so we could have a chance to talk some more."

"I like that idea. Shall we go to the park again?"

"I like that idea", Lori said with a smile.

An hour later, Tom pulled into Lori's driveway and walked her to the door.

"So do we have a date Saturday night?" Tom asked.

"Of course, but I will see you Friday night at the game."

"I can't wait", Tom said as he leaned down to kiss Lori, this time a little longer.

"Good night Tom. Sweet dreams."

"You know it", was his reply.

15

Thursday morning as Lori came down stairs; Sandy smiled and greeted her daughter, "Good Morning, Honey! Did you sleep well?"

"Oh yes I did", Lori answered with a big grin on her face. "Wasn't Tom absolutely fantastic last night?"

"He certainly was. I noticed you were really into the game."

"You know, Mom, I am beginning to like basketball a whole lot better these days!"

"Oh? Is it that you like the game better, or is it that *WHO* is playing in the game, that you are beginning to like better?"

"Ha! Ha! Ha! Well I guess a little of both. Tom is really a great guy, Mom. He is really the first guy I have ever really had any attraction for."

"Yes, Tom is a good kid. He comes from good stock! So I take it you two are going to be seeing each other again soon?"

"Oh yeah, Saturday night we have a date. But, of course, there is a game Friday night at Loraine Central. I will see him then."

"Okay, bubbly girl, in the meantime, how about some breakfast?"

"Sure. Can I help?"

"Yup, you can make some toast and set the table!"

"I can do that."

Friday evening at the game..........

Sandy and Lori arrived at Loraine Central as the JV game was getting underway. Lori spotted the Limestone varsity team seated on the far side of the gymnasium as they walked in.

"Wow! Doesn't Tom look handsome in that tie and jacket?"

"He sure does, Honey. Your father's rules you know? Players must were a tie to all away games."

They made their way to a seat. Tom, in the meantime, was oblivious to the fact that Lori was there. He was too busy chatting with his teammates and catching glimpses of the JV game to notice. It was actually his friend Larry Jones that spotted her first.

"Hey, there is Lori sitting over there," he pointed.

Tom turned to look, and there she was starring right at him and smiling. He smiled back and waved.

"Okay, Buddy. I guess you will be showing your stuff again tonight!" Larry said.

"Ah, I was just lucky the other night, that's all", Tom replied.

"Just lucky? Come on Tom. Luck didn't have a whole lot to do with it. That was some kind of performance. Face it my friend, God has given you exceptional talent. Don't deny it."

"Thank you, Larry. I needed that little scolding. You are right, I am blessed. But sometimes I feel like I am taking away from some of the other guys by stealing the limelight."

"Tom, don't feel that way. The guys on this team love it, and so does Coach Smith. Limestone hasn't had a winner here in several years. You are an answer to prayer, my friend."

"Whoa! Wow! I guess I have never looked at it that way. But I appreciate your kind words. I'll try not to let you down."

As the third quarter of the JV game ended, the varsity headed for the locker room to get dressed for their game. They came back up just in time to see the final minute of the game as Limestone eked out a one point win 54-53.

As the team was returning to the bench after the pregame warmups, Tom looked up at Lori who was just brimming. He smiled, winked and gave her a thumb up! Then he went to work!

Limestone took control of the game from the opening tip. Tom was once again brilliant with his amazing skills. He also was well aware of the open man, and handed out several assists along the way.

Leading by 16 points beginning the fourth quarter, Marv pulled all the starters, and played the reserves the rest of the game. Loraine closed to within eight, but it was too little, too late! Final: Limestone 81-Loraine 73.

Tom once again had a great night. 42 points, 14 rebounds, nine assists, seven blocked shots!

Being an away game, Tom didn't get to see Lori after the game. The team showered, boarded the bus and headed back to Limestone.

Saturday night……..

Tom pulled into the Smith's driveway at precisely 6:00 PM. After parking, he walked up to the front door and rang the doorbell. Marv answered the door.

"Ah, come on in Tom. Lori will be down in a minute. Last minute preparation you know?"

"Yes Sir."

"Just thought I'd let you know, There was a scout from Syracuse University at the game last night. I didn't talk to him, but I recognized him from previous experiences. You are being watched, Tom. That is good."

"How do you know he was watching me, Coach? Maybe he was looking at someone else?"

"Don't be ridiculous Tom. He was watching you! The word is out! I have a feeling there will be several scouts watching you soon!"

"Well, I...."

"Hi Tom", Lori spoke up as she came bustling downstairs all bright and cheery.

"Wow! You look great!" Tom exclaimed.

"What this? Just an old pair of slacks I had kicking around; nothing special!"

"Looks good to me" Tom said smiling.

"Alright, you two, get on out of here", Marv spoke up. "Have fun."

"See you later, Dad", Lori said as she gave her father a kiss on the cheek.

Tom took Lori to 'Tiffany's Restaurant' for dinner, and then headed out to the Pioneer Drive-In to see *The Great Escape*, starring Steve McQueen.

After the movie they just sat and talked until they were the last car to leave. Tom drove Lori home and spent several more minutes talking with her before walking her to the door.

"I hope you enjoyed our evening Lori."

"I did, very much so. You know that is the best movie I have seen in a long time. And it was great being with you, Tom. You are a real gentleman and I appreciate that."

"Thank you. I very much enjoy being with you Lori. Can we see each other more while you are home for the holidays?"

"Of course; I would like that."

"So would I", Tom said as he took Lori in his arms and gave her a long good night kiss.

"Good night, Tom. Sweet Dreams."

"You leave me breathless, Lori!"

"Good night, Tom", Lori said smiling as she turned and walked into the house.

Tom and Lori saw a lot of each other during the Christmas break. They attended a couple of Christmas parties, went to church together, took in another movie, and went out to eat a few times. The two and a half weeks went by far too quickly for Tom. And then it was back to school and back on the court as the team began conference play.

Limestone swept through their first two games, winning easily over Black Rock Central and East Damon High. Tom continued his magic with superb performances in both games. Local newspapers were following the team closely and college scouts were taking in the games on a regular basis. Tom Chaimberbrook was being touted as one of the premier players in the country!

Monday, January 13, 1964......

It was a cold snowy evening as Marv was putting his team through their paces getting them ready for their next game at Sauquoit Central.

As practice was finishing up, Marv and Thomas were picking up the basketballs and heading for Marv's office.

"I am a little concerned about this weather, Thomas."

"Yeah, it snowed up in the Adirondacks over the weekend and it is snowing here now. Forecast is for more snow tomorrow."

"I know, we may not be playing tomorrow. I will make a phone call in the morning to see what the weather is like before we start up there."

A minute later Larry Jones came walking in to Marv's office. "Hey Coach, I just remembered, we are having a little birthday party for my Grandma tomorrow after school. So, if you don't mind, I'll just drive up to the game instead of riding the bus."

"You know, Larry, I don't like my players driving to away games. But I will make an exception this time. As a matter of fact, we may have to postpone the game; the weather is not looking very good. I will let the team know in the morning after I make a phone call."

"Thanks, Coach. I'll see you in the morning."

That night, more snow fell in the Limestone area. But it stopped snowing early in the morning, and the day broke with beautiful sunshine and 25 degrees. At 10:00 AM Marv made a phone call to Sauquoit Central to check on the weather.

"Ah, yes, good morning Marvin, How are you doing today?" came the voice on the other end.

"Just fine Frank, I hope you are?" Marv answered the Sauquoit coach.

"I doing great, Marvin; looking forward to our game tonight."

"Well that is the reason I'm calling, Frank. I was wondering how the weather is up there in the mountains?"

"Well we had some more snow here last night but the plows were out early and got the roads cleared so we are in session today. The forecast isn't calling for any more snow until possibly late this evening or tomorrow morning. So we should be able to get the game in."

"Yeah, we had snow here last night as well, but bright sunshine right now. Okay, I will let the team know that the game is on for tonight then."

"Great; I'm looking forward to seeing that Chaimberbrook kid play tonight. He has been getting a lot of publicity lately."

"Yes he has. You will see why tonight, Frank!"

"Can't wait; See you tonight Marvin."

After the call, Marv hit the intercom button. "Attention all Varsity and JV basketball players, this is Coach Smith.

'After talking with the Sauquoit coach, the weather looks favorable for tonight's games. All players be ready to board the bus at four o'clock."

Marv, Thomas and JV coach Farmington were waiting at the door of the bus as the players were boarding. Tom approached Marv and said, "I haven't seen Larry or his brother, Coach. They should have been here well before now?"

"Ah, it's alright, Tom. Larry told me they were having a little birthday party for his grandmother tonight after school. He will be along a little later in time for the game."

"Okay, Coach. I was just a little worried when I didn't see them."

"Don't worry, Tom. Stay focused on the task at hand. We have got a game to play."

"Yes, Sir", Tom answered as he got on the bus.

Halfway to Sauquoit Central, it started to snow again. The players were hamming it up on the bus, and the coaches were busy going over their game plan, so no one paid any attention to the weather.

As the JV game progressed through halftime, outside the snow kept coming down harder.

With the game tied at 42 all at the end of the third quarter, the varsity headed for the locker room to get dressed for their game. As the team was about ready to go back to the gymnasium, Larry Jones still had not showed up. Now Marv was getting worried!

16

The team got back to the gym just as the final buzzer signaled the end of the fourth quarter. The game was tied at 56! Overtime meant a slight reprieve for Marv. *'Maybe this will give Jones a little more time to get here'*, he thought.

The game ended five minutes later, with Limestone squeaking out a 62-61 victory. The varsity teams hit the floor for their pregame warmups. Marv made the decision to start Jose Demarez in Jones' spot.

With Jones out of the lineup, Sauquoit kept the game close. Tom was having a good night, but not exceptional. At the half Limestone held a slim 43-40 lead, Tom had 19 points.

In the locker room, Marv was trying to rally his players. "We are doing just fine guys. We will be alright. Just keep playing the way you are and keep hitting those boards. Vidal, great job on those rebounds; Jose, you are doing great, keep it up; Rick, try getting open a little more. We need some outside shots, they are clogging the middle. Tom, try moving out a little further on the key; that may open up the underneath for a backdoor. Rick and Jose, be on the watch for this! Alright guys let's go get 'em!"

Early in the third quarter there was a huge collision under the boards, as four players were going after a rebound. A Sauquoit player came down hard on Vidal Holbrook's ankle!

The referees called a time out as Marv and Thomas rushed out on the floor to check on the fallen player. Holbrook was in pain and could not stand up. A stretcher was brought out and he was carried off the court to the locker room to be examined by a local doctor.

Marv inserted Steve Woods into the game to take Holbrook's place and the game continued.

Woods responded immediately, nailing three straight shots and grabbing off a couple of rebounds. His surge brought the team back to life. Tom opened up his game with some amazing shots, including a reverse slam over his opponent's head. That brought even the hometown crowd to its feet!

Jackson and Demarez started hitting from the outside, and also hit the cutter underneath on a couple of occasions. Limestone steadily pulled away, and cruised to an 81-68 victory!

Tom had a decent night with 30 points and a dozen boards. Jackson tallied 18 and Demarez had a career high 13. But Steve Woods was the game changer, hitting on 8 for 9 for 16 points and grabbing 10 rebounds in less than a half a game!

As the team boarded the bus for the trip back to Limestone, it was snowing heavily. Marv was informed that Vidal Holbrook had been taken to a local hospital to have, what appeared to be, his broken ankle reset. Now Marv was really worried! Holbrook down with an injury, Jones unaccounted for, and they still had to get the team back to Limestone in a very heavy snowstorm!

The bus driver moved along the treacherous road with extreme caution. One hour away from Sauquoit Central they came upon several red and blue lights! The driver pulled the bus to a stop as a police officer approached and walked up to the door of the bus.

"It will be just a few minutes before we can let you through", the officer told the bus driver. "There has been an accident up ahead and the wrecker is winching the car out of the ditch now."

All the players were watching the wrecker pull the car up onto the road. Suddenly Tom yelled out, "Oh, my gosh; that's Larry's car! Dad, Coach that is Larry Jones' car!"

Marv immediately got off the bus and went up to the officer. "Sir, I am Marvin Smith, the basketball coach at Limestone High. I believe that car belongs to one of my players. Can you tell me who the driver of the car is?"

"According to the license we found in his wallet, we have identified him as Larry Jones from Limestone", the officer replied.

"Identified him; what do you mean by that? Where is he now officer?"

"When the ambulance arrived here, he was still unconscious. His car skidded off the road and hit a tree. The ambulance took him to Good Samaritan Hospital in Watertown."

Just then the wrecker had Larry's car winched out and pulled to the side of the road.

"Alright you can go on now", the officer told Marv as he got back on the bus.

As the bus inched its way around the wreck, all the players were gawking out the window to get a better look. Larry's car was badly smashed in the front, with a broken windshield and a flat tire on the left side.

Marv informed the players that Larry had been taken to the Watertown hospital. He asked the team to pray and Tom started the prayer. Several others prayed as well, and Thomas concluded the prayer chain as the bus slowly rolled along towards Limestone.

It took nearly two and a half more hours to get back to the school because of the heavy snow. When they got back Marv told Thomas that he was going to Watertown to check on Larry.

"I'll go with you", Thomas said.

"Dad, I want to go too", Tom spoke up.

"No, Son. You go on home. Your mother is probably worried over us because it is getting pretty late."

"But Dad, Larry is my best friend. Please let me go with you."

"Tom, please go on home. I will update you on Larry's condition as soon as I get back. Go home and pray, Tom. I will be back as soon as we find out something."

"Alright, Dad; be careful, the roads are bad out there."

"We will, Son. Tell you mother where we are and have her call Sandy so she won't be worried."

Marv and Thomas arrived at the hospital an hour later. Marv checked in at the front desk of the emergency room. "Can you tell me where Larry Jones is?" He asked the desk clerk.

"He is in emergency surgery on the second floor", was the response. "There is a waiting room just down the hall from the OR; you can wait there for a report from Dr. Armstrong."

"Thank you", Marv answered.

They made their way to the waiting room. As they walked in, they found Lawrence and Irene Jones and their younger son Tommy.

"How is Larry?" Marv asked Lawrence.

"We are awaiting a report from the doctor", Lawrence answered. He has been in surgery for the last hour."

A minute later Dr. Armstrong entered the waiting area. "Mr. and Mrs. Jones please come with me", he said. "And yes, son you can come too."

They left the room and went with the doctor into the OR. Five minutes later Dr. Armstrong came back out. He looked badly shaken, and seemed to be in somewhat of a daze!

"Doctor", Marv stopped him. "I am Marvin Smith, Larry's basketball coach. And this is Thomas Chaimberbrook, my assistant. Please tell us, how is Larry doing?"

The doctor looked at him in bewilderment. A tear slipped from his eye. "Larry passed away a couple of minutes ago!" the doctor replied. "I did everything I could to save the young man, but his injuries were just too severe. I'm so sorry."

Silence…..

"So if you gentlemen have no further questions", the doctor continued. "It has been a very long night. I am very tired, and I am going home to bed."

"Certainly Doctor", Thomas replied. "We completely understand. Let's go Marv, let the family have this time alone to mourn."

"Yeah, you're right, Thomas. It's late and we cannot do anything here. Let's go."

The snow started letting up on their way home, but it was nearly 3:00 am before they arrived back at Limestone High.

When Thomas got back into the house, he was surprised to find Martha laying on the couch and Tom dosing off in the recliner. They both awoke up as he entered the living room.

Tom jumped up immediately. "Dad, how is Larry doing?"

"I am afraid the news is not good, Son."

"Tell me, Dad; he is going to be alright isn't he?"

"You had better sit back down, Son."

"Oh, Thomas, it is bad isn't it?" Martha asked.

"Yes. Larry passed away just moments after we got to the hospital. I'm sorry to have to give it to you this way."

"What? No this can't be, Dad, please tell me he is going to be alright!" Tom started to shake.

"He is with the LORD now, Tom; he will be alright!"

"No! No! No! This can't be Dad! I have prayed that God would make him well again. He can't be dead! Why would God let this happen?"

"We do not understand the ways of God, Son. His ways are far above our ways. But be grateful that Larry was a believer, and he is now in the arms of JESUS, OUR SAVIOUR and KING!"

"I can't take this anymore, Dad", Tom was crying and shaking. "Larry was my best friend. No! I cannot accept this." He stormed for his room.

"Tom, wait, I, I, I........."

"Let him go, Thomas", Martha spoke up. "This is very dramatic for him. Just let him calm down. This is a terrible shock for everyone. How are Lawrence and Irene taking this?"

"Marv and I left the hospital after the doctor gave us the news. We thought it best to leave them alone in their grief."

"Of course, let's try to get some shuteye. It's late."

"I'll try, but I don't think sleep will come easy tonight. I know Marv probably won't sleep at all, and Tom........."

"Just leave him alone, Thomas. You know that Tom is very mature for his age. He will be alright after he has had some time to let this entire nightmare sink in."

"I hope you are right, Martha. I hope you are right."

17

A dark cloud hung over Limestone the next morning. Partially due to the weather, it was misting snow and a cold 21 degrees, but more so as the word rapidly spread about the previous night's tragic news.

As Marv pulled into the staff parking lot at the high school, his usual time, he noticed that the American flag was flying at half-mast. Marv had not slept a wink, and he looked it. His eyes were bloodshot, he forgot to shave, his hair was not combed and he felt terrible!

He headed straight to the cafeteria. *'Coffee! I have got to have some coffee'*, he thought. He poured himself a large mug full and started to drink it.....BLACK! *'I've got to get my head out of the fog'*, he thought.

BUZZZZ! Just then the buzzer sounded for the morning announcements. Principal Haywood's voice came on over the intercom.

"Good morning students, teachers, and faculty. In case you have not yet heard, I am sorry to announce this morning that one of our varsity basketball players went home to be with the LORD last night!

'Senior Larry Jones succumbed to injuries sustained in a tragic automobile accident on Highway 68B on his way to the game at Sauquoit Central last evening.

'I ask each and every one of you to please offer up a word of prayer for Larry's family right now!"

There was complete silence throughout the building for a minute and a half.

"In lieu of what has happened, all evening activities scheduled for tonight are cancelled. A determination about Friday night's game with Palmdale High will be made after we have discussed our options with the coaches and the players.

'In the meanwhile we will operate on our regular school schedule. We will update everyone as soon as we have more information. All students report now to your first period classes."

Marv didn't have a class first period, so he went to his office and called Sauquoit Hospital to check on Vidal Holbrook. He learned that Vidal had been transferred to Good Samaritan in Watertown early that morning. So he called Good Samaritan and the receptionist transferred his call to Vidal's room.

"Hello, this is Nurse Jane Westin. May I help you?" a female voice on the other end of the line asked.

"Yes, I am trying to reach Vidal Holbrook. Do I have the correct room number?"

"Yes, Sir; shall I put him on the line?"

"This is Coach Marvin Smith calling. Is he able to talk with me?"

"Oh, yes Sir. Hold on a second."

"Good Morning Coach"; came a cheery voice.

"Vidal! Great to hear your voice! How are you doing, Partner?"

"Doing well, Coach; as it turns out, my ankle is not broken after all, just a fractured bone that will take a while to heal."

"Wow that is good news Vidal, glad to hear it. How long do they think you will be in the hospital?"

"Doctor said I may be released by tomorrow morning. They have my foot in a cast and I am under observation for today. If all goes well, I should be out of here tomorrow."

"Great news, Vidal, see you soon, take care."

There was an eerie quietness in the air at Limestone High that day. Larry Jones was not only a star athlete, but he was also a very popular student among his classmates.

Often between classes, small groups would congregate together and remember the good times with Larry. They would pray for the family, and cry on each other's shoulders.

For the first time in almost two years, Tom Chaimberbrook missed a day of school. He was so shaken that he couldn't function properly, so he stayed home and mourned all day.

Word came later that day about the funeral arrangements. Visiting hours would be Thursday evening from 6:00 to 8:00, with the funeral scheduled for 1:00 Friday afternoon.

Early the next morning, Principal Haywood told the entire student body and faculty the news and called for a special meeting with the basketball team and coaches immediately following morning announcements. The team met in the gymnasium with Marv, Thomas, JV Coach Farmington and Principle Haywood.

"I am going to leave this decision up to you, the players, on what to do about our scheduled game tomorrow evening", Haywood explained.

Tom immediately spoke up. "Well, I can only speak for myself, but I don't think I would be able to play under the circumstances. Larry was a dear friend of mine; I need more time to get through this."

The rest of the team readily agreed, and so did the coaches.

"Very well", Haywood said. I will call Palmdale High and postpone the game.

After the meeting, Tom, Rick Jackson, and Nathan Boone all volunteered their services to be pall bearers at Larry's funeral.

Friday……..

Principle Haywood suspended all afternoon classes so that students and faculty could attend the funeral. The school shut down after fourth period class at 11:45.

A huge crowd was in attendance, including all of the varsity team, dressed in ties and jackets. Most of the JV squad was there as well. Even Vidal Holbrook made it (on crutches), and sat with his teammates during the service.

Though the players were trying to act as men, most all of them broke down during the very emotional service. Tom was in tears the whole time, and was barely able to handle his pall bearing duties after the service.

Irene Jones held on tight to her younger son Tommy throughout the entire service, as both cried throughout. Lawrence, on the other hand, sat almost in a complete daze, as if in a trance.

After the gravesite service, many tried to comfort the family with words of encouragement. But Lawrence walked away, needing to escape the reality of what was happening.

Thomas noticed this, and tried to approach him with some consoling words. "Lawrence, is there anything I can do to help you through this? I know what a shock this has to be, may I pray for you right now?"

"Prayers won't do any good at this point", Lawrence snapped. "My son is dead! Why? Am I living in a fantasy? This cannot be real!"

"It is hard for us to understand the ways of GOD, Lawrence. HIS ways are far above our ways."

"HIS ways? GOD took my son! What kind of a loving GOD would do that?"

"Lawrence, it was an accident! GOD did not intentionally take your son! Be grateful that your son knew the LORD! He is with JESUS right now as we speak!"

"I know you are trying to help, Thomas. And I appreciate that. But it is hard to be grateful when you are grieving with a broken heart. I loved my son. Life will never be the same without him. I don't know if I can even go on."

"You must be strong for Irene and Tommy, Lawrence! They need you now more than ever before. Please let me pray for you, right now."

There was no reply from Lawrence, so Thomas began to pray. *"Heavenly Father: Please give peace and comfort to my friend Lawrence and his family. At times like this, we need you more than ever. Only you can bring comfort to the soul!*

'May we rest in the assurance that Larry is with you now, and someday we will all be reunited with you. Oh what a day that will be Father, when we see JESUS face to face!

'Bring comfort to us now Father, as you draw us ever closer to yourself! For it is in the precious name of JESUS that we pray. AMEN!"

With that, Thomas hugged Lawrence and walked away, leaving him standing alone.

Monday, at evening practice........

Marv called up Loren Drake from the JV team to replace Larry Woods and recalled Montgomery Alexander to fill in for Vidal Holbrook temporarily. George Farmington also informed Marv that Tommy Jones had quit the JV team, obviously over the grief of losing his brother.

Marv was inserting the new players into the mix to get them acquainted with the varsity style of play. "Okay guys, let's run the 'Rover Back Door", Marv hollered out.

Drake passed off to Jackson and cut to the right perimeter. Rick fed inside to Tom, who seemed completely unaware that the ball was coming to him. The ball bounced off his chest and trickled out of bounds.

"Okay", Marv shouted. "Let's do it again, "Rover Back Door."

Same play, this time the ball slipped right through Tom's hands and out of bounds!

"Come on Tom", Rick shouted out. "We have run this play dozens of times. You know the ball is coming to you, to bounce pass back to the cutter underneath. Let's go!"

"Sorry guys", Tom responded. "I just don't seem to be into the game. Coach, I need a break!"

With that Tom walked off the court to the water cooler.

"Nathan, take over in the pivot and let's run this play again", Marv hollered.

Tom went and sat down on the bleachers and Thomas came over to him. "Tom, I know this is hard, but it is time to snap out of it for the sake of the team. We have got a game tomorrow night with Iroquois Central, and the team needs you."

"I am sorry, Dad. Right now basketball does not seem to be at the top of the list on my mind."

"It will take time to get over Larry's death, Son. But LIFE goes on; IT IS WHAT IT IS!

"Basketball is a game, Dad. Life is fragile. I am not sure I want to play anymore. This has put a whole new perspective on things as far as I am concerned."

"Alright, Tom; you will have to figure this out on your own", Thomas said. He walked back out on the court to help Marv with practice.

18

Tuesday evening………

The team was getting dressed for their game with Iroquois Central as the JV's were finishing up their game. Rick Jackson was trying to pump the team up.

"Alright guys, this is the story. Are we going to just go through the motions, or are we going to win this game for Larry?"

Everyone was in agreement, this one was for Larry Jones, and he would want it that way!

"How about it, Tom; Are you with us?" Rick asked.

"Ah, sure", Tom answered hesitantly.

"Alright, guys, let's go get 'em", Marv encouraged the team.

Marv started Steve Woods in place of Vidal Holbrook and Jose Demarez in Larry Jones' spot.

The game started out innocent enough. Tom easily controlled the opening tap, and Jackson and Demarez both hit outside shots to get the game started. But when the ball came inside, Tom seemed unclear as to what to do. Instead of trying to penetrate the middle, he would casually pass off to a teammate.

The rest of the team responded well, with Woods and Boone helping to take up the slack. But when the first quarter ended, with Limestone in the lead by six points, Tom had yet to score! In fact he had only taken one shot!

In the huddle Marv responded. "Tom, get into the game! Where are you? We are doing okay, but it would be a whole lot easier if you were with us. Come on, Partner, get with the program!"

The pep talk helped a little, as Tom began to respond a little better, banging home a few shots here and there, but he was way off his normal game.

At halftime, while Marv was talking to the rest of the team, Thomas took Tom aside and sat him down. "Son, what can I say that will bring you out of this? Marv is perplexed as to what to do. Fortunately, we are playing pretty well as a team, but you are missing in action!"

"Dad, I am tired. I cannot concentrate on the game when my mind is still whirling over what has happened. It is like a bad nightmare, I just can't get over it. Maybe I just need to drop off the team. I am not doing anybody any good."

"Tom, don't talk like that. That would be disaster for the whole team. They look up to you; they want you to perform at your highest level. Quitting is not an option! Don't even think about it!"

When the team came out to start the second half, Tom walked over to Marv. "Coach, take me out of the game. I am just not helping at all. Nathan can handle the pivot, we will be alright."

"Alright, Tom, take a seat. If I need you I'll call on you."

With that Tom went and sat down on the far end of the bench.

The game progressed along smoothly for Limestone through the third quarter. But halfway through the final period things began to change quickly. Iroquois closed the gap to within two points as their guards starting hitting some key shots and Limestone seemed out of kilter on their defense.

When Sookie Shane, Iroquois' sharp shooting point guard, drilled a 30 footer to tie the game at 68 all, Marv called a time out!

"Chaimberbrook, get in there!" Marv hollered out, snapping Tom out of his trance at the end of the bench. All eyes were on him as he came up to the huddle

"Now look, Tom, we are counting on you", Marv began. "There is only three and a half minutes left in the game. Now I want to see you play the way I know you can. Are you up to it?"

"Yes, Sir, I'll give it a shot", Tom responded.

"Good, now we are going inside all we can, got it? And hit them boards hard, we need every rebound we can get. Let's go!"

Demarez fed into Jackson, who brought the ball up court and immediately went inside to Tom. With a quick move Tom was around his opponent and slammed it home!

That little burst brought the team out of their doldrums and they played flawlessly the rest of the way. Tom hit on four more shots and finished with 18 points, with only three and a half minutes of play in the second half!

The fans and the players were whooping it up after the game, but Tom was in his own little bubble. He quickly showered, dressed, and was out of the building in less than 10 minutes.

Most of the fans and some of the team headed over to 'Hank's' after the game as usual. Tom just wanted to be alone.

He drove over to the town park where Lori and he had spent some time together. He sat there and envisioned some of the good times that he and his friend Larry had together during the short time that they had known each other. He remembered in particularly the times that they used to pray together. This brought comfort to him, knowing that Larry was a devout Christian, and was now with the LORD. Tom sat and prayed, and cried, for over an hour. Finally he composed himself enough to drive home.

This was the hardest thing that he had ever dealt with in his young 17 years of life. *'How can I cope with this?'* He thought. *'My world has been turned upside down, how can I go on?'*

Thursday evening……..

After two terrible practices on Wednesday and Thursday evening, Tom was about ready to tell Marv that he could not play anymore. He discussed it with his father after they got home. Of course Thomas tried to talk him out of it, but Tom had his mind made up.

While they were talking in the living room, the phone rang. "Tom, it's for you", Martha called out.

Tom was eager to get out of the conversation with Thomas, so he quickly jumped up and answered the phone. "Hello?" he answered, uncertain as to whom it was.

"Hello, Tom", came a sweet voice on the other end.

"Lori! Is that you?"

"You were expecting someone else?"

"Ah, no, of course not, I am just a little surprised to hear your voice, that's all."

"Well, I thought maybe you needed a little cheering up, so I decided to give you a call."

"I must admit, this is a very pleasant surprise."

"Dad has told me what happened, Tom. I am so sorry. I knew Larry, and he was a great guy. We had some classes together my senior year. I know this has to be hard on you. You and Larry were close weren't you?"

"Very close. He was my best friend."

"Now, I want to be your best friend, Tom."

Tom started to get emotional. "Thank you, Lori", he said with a shaky voice. "I needed that assurance."

"Dad tells me that this has affected your game. What can I do to help? Do I need to come there and cheer you up?"

"Lori, you can't just take off from school and come here. I am thinking about giving up basketball anyways. As I have told you before, I enjoy the game, but there are more important things in life than basketball."

"Not at this stage in your life, Tom! Right now basketball should be THEE most important thing in your life!"

"What do you mean?" Tom asked somewhat bewildered by Lori's statement.

"I mean, you are an extremely talented player, Tom Chaimberbrook! You have an obligation to play at your highest level for the sake of the team!

'The players look up to you to be their leader. Limestone hasn't seen a champion in a long time, now is their chance. Don't let them down, Tom! Please, they are counting on you. Do it for their sake!"

"I don't know if I can, Lori", Tom trembled.

"Then if you can't do it for the team, Tom, will you do it for ME?"

"What? I don't understand, Lori. You have told me that you don't even like basketball."

"Well, it seems lately I've gotten a little more interested in the game, especially a certain player that I've taken quite a liking too!"

"Wow, you really have a way of cheering somebody up Lori, I really appreciate that."

"Not just somebody, Tom. If it weren't for you, I probably still would not be interested in basketball.

'So please, do it Tom. Play at your best; concentrate solely on the game, just as you have always done. I'll be cheering you on! You can do this! Your time is now, Tom. Tomorrow will come soon enough!"

"You speak with such maturity and wisdom, Lori. I guess that is one of the things that attract me to you the most. Thanks for calling, I really needed that. I was about ready to tell your Dad that I was going to drop off the team. You've given me a new perspective on the situation. Thank you!"

"I love you, Tom. Good night and sweet dreams."

"What did you say?"

"Good night, Tom." With that Lori hung up.

Tom slowly hung up the phone, trying to grasp what Lori had just said. *'Did she just say that she loved me?'* he thought.

He walked back into the living room smiling and with a whole new attitude! His new appearance did not escape Thomas' eye.

"Well, that phone call must have made you feel better", Thomas proclaimed.

"You know, Dad, I've changed my mind" Tom answered. "I believe I'll stick around. After all, that would be the way Larry would want it, don't you think?"

Thomas smiled and replied, "Yes, I believe that would be the way Larry would want it, Son. Not to mention the rest of the team. And I suspect a certain GIRL may want it that way too?"

"Ha! Ha! Yes, Lori does have a way with words. Well, good night, Dad, I going to bed."

"Good night, Son. I am pleased with the change in your attitude."

After Tom had left the room, Martha spoke up, "Did I not tell you that girl was a natural match for Tom, Thomas?"

"Yes, Martha, You told me. Don't rub it in!"

19

Friday evening……..

Tom's mood had changed dramatically as the team bus headed for Palmdale High. He was back to his usual self, laughing and carrying on with his teammates. Marv took notice as he mentioned to Thomas.

"Looks like that phone call from Lori last night may have had some effect on Tom's attitude, Thomas."

"Yeah, he cheered up almost instantaneously after they talked."

"Well the timing couldn't be better. Palmdale could be a challenge for us. Only one loss so far and that was to Adirondack Parochial. I hope Tom is up to the task."

"I think he is back. If he concentrates on the game, we should be fine."

"Good. I will try to get the team to keep on encouraging him. Palmdale has a big guy in the middle, so we are probably going to need a solid performance from Tom to take them. Especially on the road, we are not going to have many fans there."

"Tom likes a challenge. This should drive him to play at his best."

As the teams were finishing up their pregame warmups and heading back to their respective benches, Tom did his usual glance behind the bench to see if his mother was there. Again he was stopped dead in his tracks! There sitting between Martha and Sandy was Lori!

"What are you doing here?" He mumbled bewilderedly.

"I figured you needed some inspiration to play better", Lori said. "So I hopped on a plane this afternoon and, here I am!"

"Lori, I, I, I don't know what to say."

"Don't say anything, Tom, Just play like you mean it. We will talk later. Okay?"

"I, I, I just can't believe you are here."

"Would you rather I leave?"

"Of course not. I, I, I..."

"PLAY, Tom. Do it for ME."

Tom went back to the huddle and looked straight at Marv with intensity in his eyes. He was ready! "Let's roll guys!"

Tom took complete charge right at the offset, controlling the tap over to Rick Jackson who brought the ball quickly down court and fed it back inside. With a lightning move, Tom was around his opponent and slammed it home to start things off.

Before Palmdale could get the ball halfway back up court, Jose Damerez stole the ball from his opponent, drove straight down the lane and laid it up and in!

The Limestone defense was stifling, stopping their opponent's cold. Meanwhile the offense was blistering hot! Building up an explosive 18-0, lead with just five minutes gone in the game, Palmdale High coach Carl Wells was forced to call a timeout.

The onslaught continued. By halftime Limestone had an overwhelming 52-13 lead! Some of the hometown fans were already leaving.

Midway through the third quarter, leading by 43 points, Marv pulled all of his starters and inserted the reserves. The change in personnel made little difference, as the reserves poured it on!

Newcomer Loren Drake and Montgomery Alexander took over the backcourt duties and ran the offense almost flawlessly. Meanwhile, Fred Long stepped into the pivot, replacing Tom, and performed magnificently

When all was said and done, Limestone blew out Palmdale High 98-38, leaving the home team and their fans totally embarrassed! Tom finished with 49 points, playing in just 18 minutes of the game!

After the game, Tom met briefly with Lori and made arrangements for a date Saturday night. He couldn't wait to see her!

He pulled into the Smith's driveway at 5:30 Saturday afternoon. Lori was ready and waiting for him.

"So where are we going this evening", Lori asked as she greeted Tom with a kiss.

"There is a new Italian restaurant in Watertown call 'Gucci's'", Tom answered. "I thought maybe we would try it out."

"Sounds good. I like Italian food."

"And then, seeing we both like Steve McQueen, *THE MAGNIFICANT SEVEN*, is playing at the Palisades Theater just a few blocks from there."

"Sounds like you have the whole evening planned out already."

"More or less; Of course, that is if all of this meets with your approval?"

"Certainly, let's go."

They enjoyed a delicious meal at 'Gucci's' then went to the movies. On the way back to Limestone Tom asked, "So are we on for church tomorrow?"

"Sorry, I can't make that one. I have a 9:15 flight back to Atlanta in the morning."

"I see. Well in that case......look I know it's getting late, but we may not be seeing each other for a while. So would you mind if we go by the park for a few minutes?"

"I was wondering when you were going to ask. Certainly, that is our usual routine isn't it?"

"Well yeah, I guess it is. I am just not ready for this night to end yet."

"Nor am I, let's go."

After arriving at the park an hour later, Tom had to have an answer to a question.

"Lori, when we were talking on the phone the other night, I thought I heard you say, 'I love you'. Or maybe it was my imagination, because it was something that I was hoping you would say."

"You heard correctly, Tom. I can't explain it, but I have fallen in love with you. I have never felt this way before about anyone. There is something very special about you; something very mature about you. You are beyond your years in your thinking."

"I can honestly say the same thing about you. I love you too, Lori. Being apart like this makes me feel lonely at times. Then when Larry was killed, I really went into a deep depression. Thank you for getting me back on track. So what are we going to do?"

"For right now, you are going to keep on playing, and I am going back to school. We will see each other when we can. Don't give up basketball, Tom. I can come home almost anytime if you need me. But right now, concentrate on your game. After the season is over, we will talk about our future then. Is that fair enough?"

"You are so wise, Lori. I love you!"

"I love you too."

After another hour, Tom drove Lori home and walked her to the door.

"My gosh, it's almost two AM", Tom noticed looking at his watch. "I guess I will hear about this from Coach, keeping his daughter out all night?"

"Don't worry about "Coach", Tom. I can handle my Dad."

With that, they embraced into a long good night kiss. "Good night, Tom. I Love You. Sweet dreams."

"Good night, Lori. I Love you too. We will keep in close touch, okay?"

"Certainly; keep your chin up, Tom. Tomorrow is another day."

"AMEN. Good night, Lori."

Sunday evening……

Ralph Stevens was driving back into Limestone. He had been out of town all weekend visiting with an old friend of his that he hadn't seen in several years. There was some light snow in the air, and the temperature had dropped to 13 degrees. As he started across the Limestone Bridge, he noticed a figure leaning over the railing on the left hand side.

At first he didn't pay that much attention, but as he got closer he realized who it was.

'My God, that's Lawrence Jones', he thought. *'What in the world is he doing out here in this cold?'*

Ralph pulled across the bridge and off to the side. He shot the motor off and ran back to see if he could help.

"Lawrence, Lawrence, what are you doing out here in this cold Man? Come on I'll give you a lift."

Lawrence turned towards him, and seemingly coming out of a trance shouted, "Stay away from me Ralph! Don't come near me! Leave me alone!"

Ralph then realized that Lawrence was thinking about committing suicide!

"Lawrence, don't do this! My God, Man, what are you thinking? Please let me help you!"

"No! Stay away, Ralph! You don't know what it is like, trying to live without my son! I can't go on. Every time I see someone playing basketball, it reminds me of Larry! I can't take this anymore!"

"Lawrence, be reasonable. You have a wife and another son to consider. And, yes, I do know how you feel! I too have lost a son!"

That statement seemed to get Lawrence's attention. "You have? Are you trying to yahoo me Ralph?"

"No, Lawrence. It's true. My son was just 17 when he was killed in a car accident; same age as Larry. Please, Lawrence, come with me and let me help you through this."

"Where are we going, Ralph?"

"Come on, we can go over to Hank's Diner and have a cup of coffee and talk about this."

"Alright, Ralph. But you had better not be trying to Shang High me or telling me a tale. I had my mind made up when I came out on this bridge, and I still might do it!"

Ralph helped Lawrence back to his car and they drove over to Hank's Diner. After getting seated in a private booth towards the back, the waitress came over.

"What can I do for you gentlemen this evening?" she asked.

"A cup of coffee and a burger and fries for me", Ralph spoke up.

"I'll have a cup of coffee, as well", Lawrence said. "And maybe a grilled cheese sandwich and fries."

"Coming right up gentlemen. I will be right back with your coffee."

"So tell me about your son, Ralph. I didn't know you had a son?"

"Oh, yes. I lost my son about three years ago now. It still hurts when I think about it."

"Here you are gentlemen", the waitress interrupted. "Piping hot, fresh brewed coffee. Your order will be up in a few minutes."

"Thank you", Ralph said, and then he continued. "You see, Lawrence, my son was into fast cars and drag racing. He had a '55 Chevy souped up to the hilt!

'After blowing out all the local competition here he went for bigger game. He tried out Watertown, and couldn't find any competitors there either. So he decided to see what Syracuse had to offer.

'One Saturday night he found more than he could handle!"

"Here you are Gents", the waitress said bring their orders. "And, of course, a bottle of ketchup." She refilled their coffee cups. "Anything else right now?" she asked.

"That will be all for now", Ralph said.

"What happened then?" Lawrence asked.

"Well he ran across some others that had some pretty hot cars as well. I learned later, from a friend of his who witnessed the whole thing that four of them lined up on Salina Street to see who was the fastest.

Shortly after they took off, one of them sideswiped another, which threw him into another, then into another. Next thing, two cars went off on either side of the road up onto the sidewalk and slammed into a building! Two other cars went tumbling over and over down the street!

When they all came to a stop, all four of them were killed including my son. He was the youngest, just 17 years old."

"You know, Ralph, now that I recall, I remember reading about that in the newspaper. But I had no idea that any of those young men was your son. I am sorry."

"No need to apologize, Lawrence. Most people around here didn't connect that accident with my son. But I know exactly how you feel. I have been there; you can never get over it."

"So tell me, what did you do?"

"I am afraid I didn't handle it very well either, Lawrence. I already was drinking a lot, and that just drove me deeper into misery. I drank heavily for almost a year after that, trying to take my mind off of everything. I finally realized that all that was doing was driving me deeper into depression.

'Oh yes, I even had thoughts of suicide myself. But thanks be to GOD, an old friend of mine, whom we are both familiar with, Marvin Smith, came along and tried to comfort me. He got me to stop drinking. Later Thomas Chaimberbrook got me going back to church. It changed my life. You can do this too, Lawrence. Think about your family. Go talk to you pastor. He can help you through this."

"You are right, Ralph. Thank you for taking this time with me. If you hadn't come along when you did, I could be floating in the Limestone River right now."

"Come on, Lawrence. I'll take you home. Get some sleep. Tomorrow will look brighter."

20

Monday evening, Vidal Holbrook was back practicing with the team. Marv was impressed with what he saw and decided to reactivate Vidal for Tuesday night's game.

To make room for Holbrook on the active roster, Marv had to send someone back down to the JV squad. Montgomery Alexander had been very impressive filling in as a temporary while Holbrook was out with his injury. So Marv decided to send freshman Stu Baker back down to get a little more work with the JV's.

The team continued it flawless playing. Everyone jelled together, and they played like a well lubricated machine. Tom was again playing magnificently, which inspired the rest of his teammates as all of them seemed to pick it up a notch.

They breezed through the remainder of the first half of conference play virtually unscathed. When the second half began, Limestone was everybody's number one target. But the more teams focused on stopping Tom, the better everyone else played! They slid through February unbeaten, winning the Conference Championship.

Then it was on to the Sectionals where they toppled everyone handily. The next step was the Northern Regional, where they once again would have to face arch-rival Adirondack Parochial.

The game was being played in Watertown's War Memorial Coliseum and radio station WATR was on hand for the broadcast.

"Good evening, ladies and gentlemen, and welcome to an exclusive WATR broadcast of tonight's Northern Regional Championship. Tonight's game will bring together two arch-rivals, the undefeated Limestone High Raiders and the once defeated and defending Northern Regional Champion, Adirondack Parochial Monarchs.

'I'm Paul Paulson, your play- by- play announcer for tonight's game, along with Jim Jacobs your expert color analysis and commentator. And Jim it looks like we are in for a real barn burner treat tonight!"

"Yes, Paul this should be quite a match-up. Limestone coming into this game unbeaten and riding on the coattails of their superstar center Tom Chaimberbrook. Ironically, Adirondack's only loss this season came at the hands of this very Limestone team in their first game of the season. So this could be somewhat of revenge game for Adirondack.

'Now, of course, Limestone has played remarkably well, in spite of that tragic loss of their senior starting guard Larry Jones back in early January. Jones, as most of you fans will recall, was tragically killed in a horrible automobile accident on his way to a game at Sauquoit Central on that snowy cold night. But the team has rallied in spite of that traumatic circumstance and has played brilliantly since then.

'No one can escape the fact that Tom Chaimberbrook is perhaps the most sought after high school player in the nation right now either. I understand that at least two dozen colleges and universities would like to have his services next year, Paul"!

"That's right, Jim. So with that in mind, what will be Adirondack's strategy to try and stop Chaimberbrook in tonight's game?"

"Well I expect that they will try to clog up the middle and perhaps double team Chaimberbrook if they can. But, of course, that will open up the perimeter for Limestone's sharp shooting guards, so we will have to wait and see just how well that all works out."

"Alright, Jim; Folks we will be right back with tonight's starting lineups right after a word from our sponsor."

As the teams were going through their final pregame tune-ups, Marv and Adirondack coach Phil Phillips were chatting at center court.

"Somehow I had feeling we would be seeing each other again before the season was over", Marv was saying to Phillips.

"You know, Marvin, I think that first game loss actually jolted this team into realizing they have got to play every game hard to win. I want to thank you for waking them up. Now we will see how well they respond to that loss."

"Ah, Phil, I told you that you would be here. I have seen you in action enough to know the kind of coach that you are. Now the real challenge is to see which one of us can go to the Final Four."

"Well, I can tell you from experience, it does not get any easier. As you know we have been there the past two years, and have failed to get past the semi-finals."

Just then WATR came back on the air.

"Now folks, here are the starting lineups for tonight game. First for Adirondack Parochial; at the guards will be six foot senior Ronnie Johnson and 5 feet 11 inch junior Jeremy Phillips. At center is 6 foot 7 inch senior Jeffery Davidson. And at the forwards will be 6 foot 6 inch senior Michael Sweeny and 6 foot 5 inch junior Chad Shumway. The coach for Adirondack is Phil Phillips.

'Now for Limestone High; at the guards will be six foot junior Rick Jackson and 5 foot 10 inch sophomore Jose Demerez. At center is 6 foot 8 inch Tom Chaimberbrook. And at the forwards will be 6 foot 7 inch sophomore Vidal Holbrook and 6 foot 4 inch junior Nathan Boone. The coach for Limestone is Marvin Smith."

"Big crowd on hand tonight", Jacobs chimed in. "And they are still coming in as we get ready to get underway. Take it away Paul."

"Alright, here we go! The ball is up and Chaimberbrook controls the tap over to Jackson who deliberately brings the ball down court. He is looking inside but Adirondack has the middle clogged. Jackson flips over to Demerez. Demerez takes a couple of bounces and flips back to Jackson. Quick throw to the inside. Chaimberbrook fakes to his left and bounces backhanded to the cutter underneath, reverse layup up and in! Jose Demerez sneaking in the back door for the first two points of the game."

"Nice move by the sophomore", Jacobs jumped in. "That is what Marvin Smith refers to as the 'Back Door Rover' play. Well executed by the Raiders."

"Shumway feeds in to Johnson. He brings the ball up court quickly. Over to Phillips, quick throw inside. Davidson tries to hook over Chaimberbrook, it's blocked! Out to Jackson, long throw down court to the speeding Demerez. He lays it up and in and is fouled!

'Foul is on Phillips. Demerez sinks the free throw and the Raiders take a 5-0 lead.

'Shumway feeds in again to Johnson who slowly brings the ball up court. Over to Phillips, quick throw to Sweeney driving the base line. He shoots over Holbrook, good and he is fouled!

'Free throw is good. Boone inbounds to Jackson, over to Demerez. Stolen by Phillips, who drives the lane and lays it! And the Monarchs are right back in this game!"

"Great hands by Phillips," Jacobs jumped in. Caught Demerez completely off guard and tied this game up a five all!"

"Jackson brings the ball back down court, glancing at Coach Smith. Smith is holding up some fingers, indicating a play. Jackson fires in to Boone who sets a pick, hands back to Jackson for a 20 foot jumper. Good!"

"This is what we talked about earlier, Paul," Jacobs again jumped in. "Clogging the middle opens up the perimeter for the guards. And the Limestone guards know how to find the hole!"

"Indeed they can Jim. Let's see how Adirondack reacts to that. Shumway inbounds to Johnson. Long throw down to Sweeney. He shoots from 18 feet, no good, rebound Chaimberbrook. He tosses out to Demerez, quickly down court to Jackson. He drives the lane and lays it up, off the rim no good. Rebound by Holbrook the trailer, who slams it home!"

"Listen to that crowd, Paul. That slam brought them to life! Boy you can feel the excitement in this coliseum; it feels like the building is shaking!"

"Here come the Monarchs back up court. Johnson feeds off to Phillips over to Sweeney, back to Phillips for a 20 foot jumper, yes! And he was fouled by Demerez.

'Phillips adds the extra point and here come the Raiders. Jackson brings it up court, he looks inside. The middle is still jammed up. Into Boone on the left flank; Lightning pass to Chaimberbrook at the top of the key, he shoots from 15 feet, Yes!"

"Wow, what great athletic ability by the Raiders superstar", Jacobs volunteered. "He not only is absolutely amazing from inside the circle, but, as you seen right there, he can also come outside and nail that short jumper with ease. This is why scouts from all over the country are looking at him. He is a valued commodity to say the least."

The two teams traded baskets back and forth through the remainder of the first period, with Limestone taking a three point lead. As the second quarter began, Coach Phillips changed his defensive strategy from a clog in the middle to a straight man-to-man. Marv quickly recognized this and had the guards go inside. Tom then went to work!

"And there he goes again!" Paul Paulson was screaming into the microphone. "A sweeping left hand hook over Davidson is good and this crowd is going absolutely bananas!"

"Well, that shift in the Monarchs defense really opened it up for Chaimberbrook", Jacobs commented. "He is almost impossible to stop when he has free reign underneath."

"Time out Adirondack! Phillips has got to try to put something else together to stop Chaimberbrook if he can; Limestone by a dozen, 38-26 midway through the second.

'Here come the Monarchs back up court. Phillips over to Johnson; quick pass Shumway, he shoots a 15 footer from the base line. Off the rim, rebound Sweeny, he puts it back up. Blocked by Chaimberbrook!

'Over to Holbrook, outlet pass to Demerez speeding down court. He drives the lane and lays it up and in! Phillips is screaming at his team from the sidelines."

"Phil Phillips is not a very happy camper right now", Jacobs offered in an obvious understatement.

Limestone continued their rampage as they closed out the half leading 53-37.

As the second half got underway, Phillips tried another strategy; a collapsing zone defense that boxed off the middle when the ball came inside. It worked for a while. Tom was shut down for half off the third quarter, and Adirondack took advantage of it, closing the gap to within nine at 59-50.

"Time out Limestone", Paulson stated. "Well it looks like we are going to have a ball game here after all, Jim."

"Yes, that collapsing defense is really giving Limestone fits right now. They can't get the ball inside to Chaimberbrook and the guards have temporarily gone cold. Let's see what Marvin Smith comes up with here to try to open this game back up."

"Well it looks like we are going to have some substitutions to start with. Let's see, senior Steve Woods is coming in for Vidal Holbrook, sophomore Loren Drake is in for Jose Demerez and Fred Long in for Nathan Boone."

"Looks like Smith is giving a few of the starters a quick breather right here, to have them fresh for the stretch", Jacobs offered.

"Alright here we go again. That's Drake feeding into Jackson who brings the ball down court slowly. He feeds down the left flank to Long; quick toss out to Chaimberbrook near the top of the key. He shoots from 18 feet, yes!"

"Can't stop Chaimberbrook from anywhere around the top of the key", Jacobs observed.

As the final period got underway, Adirondack went to a full court pressure press against Limestone and kept it close, even closing the gap to within four with just under four minutes remaining.

"Time out Limestone", Paulson exclaimed. "73-69 Limestone with 3:52 left on the clock. Boy, we have seen a real thriller here tonight, Jim."

"We certainly have, Paul; Adirondack playing like the great defending Northern Regional Champion that they are, and Limestone threatening to take that title away from them. This game has had all the excitement that it was built up to be, and it looks like it could go right down to the wire!"

"Both teams back on the court now with the original starters and here we go! Boone, under tremendous pressure from Sweeney, gets it into Jackson who slowly brings the ball down court.

'Jackson looking inside for Chaimberbrook who is covered up; quick flip into Boone, he sets a pick for Jackson who shoots from 15 feet. Off the rim and rebounded by Davidson. Snap outlet to Phillips on the fast break, he drives the lane and lays it in and is fouled by the trailer Demerez!"

"That's going to be it for Demerez, Paul", Jacobs jumped in. "That's his fifth foul. And he will be replaced by Drake."

"Phillips drills the free throw, and Adirondack has cut the lead to one. 73-72 with three minutes exactly left on the clock."

"This crowd is on its feet, Paul. The noise in this building is almost deafening!"

"Indeed, Jim. What a ball game we have seen tonight. Boone gets it in, again under full court pressure from Sweeney, to Drake. Over to Jackson who brings it down court quickly. He drills it inside to Chaimberbrook. Fake left, back right and bounce pass underneath to the driving Drake who swoops under with a reverse layup. Yes! And he is fouled by Davidson!"

"Whoa! Bad news for Adirondack", Jacobs exclaimed. "Number five for Davidson. Let's see who will replace him. Davidson rarely comes out of the game so this may be the pivotal turning point right here, Paul"

"Looks like George Lancaster, a seldom used 6' 10" freshman, will replace Davidson."

"Yes, Paul, Lancaster has not played much this season and is coming in at a very critical time right now. There has to be a lot of pressure on the young freshman, especially going up against the likes of Tom Chaimberbrook."

"Alright, Drake sinks the free throw and Limestone is back up by four 76-72.

'Philips feeds into Johnson; bringing the ball up quickly. Straight into Lancaster; stolen by Chaimberbrook! Out to the speeding Drake on the fast break! He drives the lane and easily lays it in!"

"Tremendous speed from that sophomore who is playing in just his first year of basketball", Jacobs jumped in.

"Time out, Adirondack", Paulson exclaimed. "Coach Phillips is irate over there on the sidelines, Jim."

"The Monarchs are in deep trouble right now, Paul. Under two minutes to play and six behind, Phillips has got to come up with something fast to get his team back into the game."

"The momentum has certainly changed in Limestone's favor. Let's see how the Monarchs react.

'Limestone has gone to a full court press and Phillips cannot get the ball in! He flings it over Boone to Sweeney who passes off to Shumway. Shumway pivots and is called for traveling!

'Boone will inbound for Limestone at half court; into Jackson, and immediately into Chaimberbrook who spins past Lancaster and slams it home!"

"Wow, it sounds like an explosion has gone off in here, Paul", Jacobs inserted with excitement. "This Limestone crowd has gone crazy, and Coach Phillips is completely frustrated at the sudden turn of events!"

"Shumway will attempt to get it in for Adirondack, with the pressure still being applied by Limestone. He gets it into Johnson, over to Phillips, stolen by Drake! He fires back to Holbrook, and Holbrook drives and slams! And is fouled by Lancaster!"

"Pandemonium has set in here at the Watertown Coliseum, Paul. I can barely hear you and I'm sitting right beside you!"

"Yes, Jim, it is a little loud in here", Paulson responded with an overly stark understatement.

"Holbrook at the line; He shoots and misses; rebound by Chaimberbrook who slams it home again, and is fouled by Lancaster!"

"Unbelievable", Jacobs responded. "What was a barn burner of a game just a minute or so ago has turned into a rout; absolutely amazing!"

"Chaimberbrook swishes the free throw, and Limestone backs off the full court pressure allowing Shumway to get it into Johnson easily.

'Johnson in no hurry now, trailing by 13 with just 49 seconds left, this game is all but over! Johnson throws over to Phillips who fires down the right sideline to Sweeney who shoots from the corner. Off the front of the rim, rebound Chaimberbrook.

'Over to Boone on the side and up to Jackson, who holds the ball. As the clock is ticking down, Jackson is just standing in place dribbling with no real pressure from Johnson who is guarding him.

'Three seconds left; Jackson lets it fly from 30 feet. Yes! And the Limestone crowd storms the court!"

21

The following weekend Lori flew home from Atlanta. She wasn't about to miss Tom playing in the State Final Four. It was Limestone's first ever appearance and it was also another proud moment for Lori; her Dad was the one who enabled this accomplishment to become a reality.

The Final Four was being played at Syracuse University's Manley Field House, and for the first time ever, all four teams entered the competition undefeated. According to the draw, Limestone would face Southern Regional Champion Brigadier Lee High School out of Binghamton, who had upset defending Champion St. Anthony's of Long Island.

Limestone was scheduled to play in the first game. The team arrived three hours before game time. Marv wanted to get the team on the floor and give them a good feel of the court before the game. Most of his young players had never been inside Manley and the awesomeness of playing inside the famous Dome was somewhat overwhelming.

After a short workout, Marv excused the team until it was time to play. Tom was able to get together with Lori for just a little while. As they embraced each other Tom was first to speak.

"Boy I sure have missed you, Lori. I'm so glad you came to see this."

"I wouldn't have missed this for the world, Tom. It has been too long since we've been together. And I've missed you terribly too."

"What do you say we sneak out of here and go somewhere?"

"Nope; you have a game to play, my dear. First things first; win this Championship, and then we will talk about our future."

"Awe, Lori, I just want to be with you!"

"Tom, not now, later. I have been hearing about how well you have been playing and I want to see you in action. Now are you going to let me down?"

"Of course not; I will always play my best for you."

"Good, now get out there and show everyone just how good you are."

"Yes Madam, I will do my best."

They kissed once again and Tom headed for the dressing room.

With a large Limestone contingent spurring them on and Tom preforming magnificently, Limestone derailed Brigadier Lee handily, winning 84-69.

They moved on the next day to the State Championship. Their opponent was Buffalo Anchorage High who had defeated Albany's Franklyn Mills Academy in overtime in the nightcap the day before.

This was no doubt going to be the toughest assignment Limestone had faced all season. Both teams entered the game 30-0. But Anchorage High featured seven footer Carl Stone at center! Stone, like Tom, was also a top high school senior being sought after by several colleges. Tom, at 6'8" was at a severe disadvantage. This was going to be a real challenge!

Marv, gathering his team together in the locker room prior to heading into their biggest game in school history, addressed the team.

"Well guys, this is it! We have worked hard all season for this game. We are now here! Are we going to let it all go to waste now?"

"Not a chance, coach", Rick Jackson spoke up. "We made a vow after Larry Jones was killed, that we would win the next game for him. We did.

'Then we said we would win the Conference title for him. We did. Then we said we are going to the Final Four for him. We did. Now we are going to win it all for him. Ain't that right gang?"

Everyone agreed whole heartedly.

"That's the attitude I like to see", Marv said. "We have one obstacle to overcome, and it is a big!

'Seven foot big to be exact; now listen. Tom, I know you have never faced anyone like Carl Stone. But they had a tough game last night with Franklyn Mills Academy, so I am betting they are a little tired. We need to take advantage of that if we can. We will try to put pressure on the big guy when we can and try to get him in foul trouble. Everybody hit the boards hard! We are going to need every rebound we can get. Look for the open man. Rick and Jose, keep the ball moving. We want an up tempo game that hopefully will wear them down. Any questions?"

"Are we going to play man defense?" Nathan Boone asked.

"No, we will start out with a zone. They have quite a height advantage on us, so I believe a zone would be better. We may go to a box-and-one if we need to. We'll see how it goes. Any more questions? No? Alright let's do it!"

As the team returned to the bench after their pre-game warmups, Tom instinctively glanced up behind the bench. There was his Mom and Mrs. Smith with Lori sitting between them. She gave Tom a big smile and a thumb up. Tom smiled, and sat down.

As the game got underway, Stone controlled the opening tip and Anchorage scored quickly on an 18 foot jumper from the right side of the key by their star guard Willie Olsen.

Boone fed into Jackson who brought the ball up court quickly. He fed inside to Tom, who grabbed the ball and stepped forward at the same time. This move forced Stone to come out just as Tom turned to the basket and hooked left handed over Stone's head.

Stone deflected the ball but was called for a foul. Tom sank both free throws and hurried back down court.

On Anchorage's next play they forced the ball inside to Stone who whirled to the basket. But Tom held his ground and Stone was called for charging.

The strategy was working! Two minutes into the game and Stone already had two fouls on him!

Boone fed in again to Jackson, over to Demerez, long pass to Holbrook on the right flank. Vidal set a pick and Demerez fired from 15 feet on the baseline. Deflected by Stone but Tom grabbed it and slammed it home!

Anchorage seemed stunned by the play and were caught napping when Demerez intercepted the inbounds pass and drove the lane to lay it in! Limestone fans were going wild, Anchorage fans fell silent.

Anchorage again brought the ball down court. Looking to break the Limestone zone they started to slowly move the ball around in an obvious delay tactic. Unable to penetrate they tried to force the ball inside again to Stone.

When Tom seen the ball coming and reached around Stone to deflect it, Stone slapped him on the hand and was called for a foul, his third! Anchorage coach Tom Whalen went ballistic, jumping up and down and hollering at the referees. Bad move! Whalen was called for a technical!

Rick Jackson calmly sank the technical. Tom then stepped to line for a one-and-one and dropped both free throws through. Whalen was forced to take Stone out of the game. And Limestone still held possession after the technical!

Boone fed into Chaimberbrook under Limestone's own basket. He immediately slammed another one home! Four minutes into the game, Limestone had an 11-2 lead and Carl Stone was on the bench with three fouls on him! The Marvin Smith strategy was quickly paying off!

Limestone rampaged Anchorage in the first half building a 42-20 lead going into halftime. Coach Whalen had no choice but to start Stone again in the second half. Marv changed the defense strategy again, still going with the zone, but pulling Tom out to the top of the key, thus making it more difficult for the Anchorage guards to get the ball inside.

The strategy was again a stroke of genius! Anchorage was unable to go inside so were forced to take long outside shots. When they did, the Limestone zone collapsed on Stone, forcing him outside and Boone, Holbrook and Tom were able to retrieve several rebounds.

Stone was never a threat, and fouled out early in the fourth quarter with Limestone in a commanding lead at 62-38. With 4:10 left in the game, Marv pulled all of his starters and let the reserves play the rest of the game, allowing them to experience playing in a Championship game.

Final score: Limestone 70, Anchorage 50. Limestone was the only undefeated team in the state that season and the town celebrated for weeks afterwards.

What happened next?

Well, in July of 1964, Lori Smith became Lori Chaimberbrook. The couple was married at the local church where both Tom and Lori's parents attended. All of Tom's teammates attended the wedding as well as many others of his friends. Lori had several of her friends in attendance, including her bridesmaids from college.

Over two dozen colleges were recruiting Tom, and he decided to go to Kansas and play under new coach Ted Owens. Owens had just replaced Dick Harp who had resigned at the end of the season. Tom chose Kansas because he was a big fan of the great Wilt Chamberlain who played there under Harp.

Lori transferred the credits that she had earned from Georgia Tech to Kansas so the couple could be together. In the meantime, Marvin Smith accepted a head coaching position at Grossman State University, just outside of Atlanta, Georgia.

Limestone High School then offered Thomas Chaimberbrook the head coaching job, which he accepted. He immediately coaxed his old friend Ralph Stevens into being his assistant (still a volunteer position).

As Time Goes On..........

PART TWO

Thirty-Seven Years Later

July 2001

22

"Are you sure this is the right place, Tom? Nothing looks familiar to me", Lori Chaimberbrook was asking her husband as he drove along.

"Yeah, it doesn't look like I remember it either. But that sign back there said LIMESTONE-unincorporated. Maybe I am on the wrong road; after all it has been years since we have been in this part of the country. There is a service station up ahead, I'll pull in there and see where we are. I need some gas anyway."

Tom pulled their 1998 Winnebago Motor Home up to the pumps and got out to pump the gas. Meanwhile Lori went inside to pick up a pack of Nabs and get a soda.

After pumping the gas, Tom went inside to discover Lori talking to a young man at the checkout.

"Tom, this young man says that this is Limestone and we are on the right road", Lori explained.

"Yes Sir. That is correct", the cashier said. "However I am only 18, so I don't really remember how this town was before the '78 quake."

"The '78 quake?" Tom asked puzzled. "What do you mean by that?"

"Oh, my grandfather, Fred Long, has told me the story about a great earthquake here in Limestone that took place back in 1978."

"Did you say your grandfather was Fred Long? I used to play basketball with a Fred Long many years ago. Could this be the same Fred Long?"

"Oh, yes Sir. Granddad has told me about the great teams they had here back in the early '60s."

"Well, I'll be. My name is Tom Chaimberbrook young man", Tom said holding out his hand. "And yours?"

"Wow! Yes, the great Tom Chaimberbrook", the young man said excitingly, as he shook Tom's hand. "Granddad has told me many stories about you. My name is Jimmy Long. I'm filling in for a few days here while my folks are on vacation. I am so pleased to meet you!"

"And this is my lovely wife Lori", Tom said introducing Jimmy to his spouse.

"Pleased to meet you Madam", Jimmy replied shaking Lori's hand.

"So tell me, is your grandfather still around", Tom asked.

"If you are asking if he is still living, the answer is yes. But he is not around here. Granddad and Mammy moved to Florida several years ago.

'He owns a service station, convenience store, in Ocala. That's where my folks have gone for a while."

"I see; I was hoping maybe I could get to see him, but maybe at a later date. Well, nice to have met you Jimmy, we will be on our way now."

"Oh, Mr. Chaimberbrook, if you are interested in what really happened to Limestone, I can put you onto a local resident who lived here at the time. He knows the story about what really happened to Limestone."

"Really; who might that be?"

"His name is Ralph Stevens. He lives just a little way from here."

"Ralph Stevens? I know him. He was a good friend of my Dad. Where does he live?"

"Continue on down this road for about a half mile and turn right on North Road. He lives in the third house on the left"

"Thanks Jimmy. Say hello to your grandfather for me when you see him."

"Will do, Sir; he will be excited to know that I actually met the great Tom Chaimberbrook!"

Tom drove to the directions that Jimmy had given him. Pulling into the driveway, he saw an elderly man rocking away in a rocking chair on his front porch. Tom got out of the camper and approached him.

"Well, hello there, Sonny", the man smiled. "Bet you are lost. Looking on how to get to Cape Vincent?"

"No, Sir", Tom answered. "I'm looking for a Ralph Stevens."

"You have found him", Ralph replied. "What can I do for you?"

"I know you probably don't recognize me Ralph, it has been a long time. I'm Tom Chaimberbrook."

"Well I'll be", Ralph said surprised as he rose from his chair to greet Tom. "It sure has been a long time."

The two men shook hands and then Ralph said, "And who is that you have with you? Is that the beautiful former Lori Smith?"

"It is indeed, Ralph. Honey c'mon over here and let's get reacquainted with our old acquaintance."

"Ralph it's so good to see you again", Lori said as she approached them and held out her hand.

Ralph gently took her hand and said, "You are just as beautiful as you have ever been, my dear. As a matter of fact, I believe you are even prettier now than when you two got married."

"Ah, Ralph, you always was one with great compliments. Thank you!"

"Please, sit down, both of you. Can I offer you some freshly made ice tea?"

"That would be great, Ralph", Tom said. "It is a little warm out here today."

"I'll be right back. Make yourself to home."

Ralph returned a couple of minutes later with three large glasses of ice tea.

"Oh, thank you Ralph, you're so kind", Lori said.

"MMMM, that hits the spot. Thanks Ralph", Tom added.

"No problem. So tell me what brings you back to Limestone?"

"Well we had a couple of weeks off, so we decided to come back and see how much things has changed", Tom said. "And, boy have they changed! What happened to this town, Ralph? It is nothing like I remember it being when we left here several years ago."

"Well I will tell you what happened, but first I want to know a little more about you. I followed your collegiate career at Kansas, but then I lost track of you. I can't believe there was not any pro team that was not interested in you."

"Well actually there were several that seemed to be interested. It was I who decided not to play pro ball, Ralph.

'You see, by the time we graduated from Kansas, we already had two children. I did not want to be gone for long periods of time without my family, nor did I want to drag them all over the country while I was playing ball. So I turned down all the offers I had to play pro.

'Instead I used the degree I received in engineering and landed a job with Brown and Wilkinson Bridge Construction as a designer and a construction foreman. And I have to tell you, it has been a great career. Great company to work for, excellent pay, good benefits, I couldn't be happier."

"How about you, Lori, what did you do after college?" Ralph asked.

"Well, in addition to raising four children, I majored in computer science and had a few jobs in that field developing computers and writing programs for them. It has been a pretty exciting career; computers have come a long way, since my college days. I don't believe the world could live without them now."

"You got that right", Ralph stated. "I'm afraid we wouldn't be able to function nowadays without them.

'So tell me now about your folks. Last I knew, Tom, your folks were in Texas. Are they still there?"

"Yep, they are still in Texas. They left Limestone, as you know, a couple of years after Dad was elevated to head coach here."

"I remember vividly", Ralph jumped in. "Principle Haywood offered me the head coaching job when you father left, but I didn't feel qualified enough to take on that responsibility, so I turned him down."

"Well, they moved to Texas to be closer to Mom's parents who were in sort of poor health at the time. Dad got a job as an oil rigger out in the Gulf, and did that for a few years. Then the company moved him into the front office, where he worked as an Exploratron in Search and Research for new oil wells. He did that until he retired in 1986. Then he actually did go to work briefly for the Federal Government again! As an Army Recruiter! He gave that up after a couple of years, and retired for good then."

"Lori, I know your Dad, moved on to Grossman State when he left here, and then, if I recall, he went to the ABA after that?"

"That's right, Ralph, but not as a head coach. He got on as an assistant with the old Kentucky Colonels of the American Basketball Association. Dad loved that fast paced style of basketball; the 3 point basket, the red-white-and blue balls, the run and gun offense, high scoring games; he was doing what he loved to do. There probably was a good chance that he would have been their next head coach. Unfortunately, the team disbanded in 1976 when the ABA merged with the NBA.

'That left Dad without a job. It took him almost two years before he could find another coaching job. He finally went back to coaching at a high school in Georgia for four years, then retired. He and Mom still live in Woodstock, just north of Atlanta."

"Well, thanks for bring me up to date, I kind of lost track of everybody several years ago. Would you two like some more ice tea?"

"No not for me, Ralph, thanks", Tom answered.

"I'm good, Ralph, thanks", Lori spoke up.

"Okay. Well you asked me what happened to Limestone. So here is the story.......

23

'You see we had an earthquake here, one cold February winter night, back in 1978", Ralph began. "Heck, most of us were sleeping at the time, this happened around 1:30 or so in the morning. Not much going on 'at that hour of the night, so most were not even aware that an earthquake was going on.

'What got everybody's attention was when we started hearing all the sirens going off. It kind of woke everybody up wondering what in tarnation was going on. I looked out my bedroom window and all I could see was a giant ball of fire across the whole town.

'I leaped out of bed and scrambled into some clothes and rushed outside to get a better look. And boy, I'll tell you it was cold out there! Temperature must have been down around zero or below!

'I saw fire trucks and police cars coming and going from all directions. I just stood there for several minutes, almost in a daze; I couldn't believe what I was seeing.

'A few minutes more went by, then a police officer pulled into my driveway and warned me that I may want to evacuate my house as the fire was moving in this direction.

'I hesitated at first, but as the fire kept creeping closer I realized the danger that I could be in. So I rushed back into the house and grabbed a few items, threw them into the car, and headed out of town.

'I went and stayed at a friend of mine, up in Black River, for a couple of days, waiting for the firefighters to get the fire under control"

"Wow", Tom broke in. "That must have been some kind of fire."

"Oh, yes indeed it was", Ralph continued. "It was a 'seven alarm fire'. Fire companies from several nearby towns came to help put it out. It took two days to get the fire out, and it was another day before the police would let the locals back into town. They had to make certain that the situation was under control.

'When they finally did let us back in to assess the situation, it was heartbreaking. I was one of the lucky ones. Very little damage had been done to my house, so I was able to rebuild and remain here.

'Most people were not that fortunate. Over half the people in this town lost everything they had. They had no home to go back too! Business owners lost everything. Virtually every business in town was destroyed. It was very sad. A dark cloud hung over Limestone for a long time.

'It took the insurance companies over three months to settle all the claims.

'When all was settled and done, in came the construction equipment. There was no hope for rebuilding for most of the residents. People left in droves, and scattered all over the country.

'The heavy duty machines dug a large crevice that was actually started by the earthquake; and just started pushing all of the debris into the pit, and then they buried it. It took another three months to get everything cleaned up.

'A few stayed and rebuilt, but the town was so devastated that after a while, most of them also left.

'In time though, new people moved into the area. The town started to grow again and you can see where we are today. It certainly is not what you remember, but far different from those days many years ago."

"Ralph, what started the fire?" Tom asked. "Was it just the earthquake that set something on fire, or what?"

"Well what actually happened, we found out later after fire investigators finished their work that the fire actually started, of all places, in the high school building!

'They surmised that the earthquake caused the large water heater in the basement of the school to explode! When it did, of course, it set the school on fire! The fire spread rapidly due to a brisk wind that was blowing that night.

'That, and because of the fact that it happened at the time of night that it did, it took several minutes for the fire company to react.

'By the time they did, the fire had already engulfed several buildings. A call for help went out, but it took other companies several minutes, even hours for some, to get here. That is why it took so long to get the fire under control."

"Wow, what an incredible story", Tom said. "And we didn't know anything about it."

"Well, other than here locally and in New York State itself, the news never went very far. I guess the national media didn't think it was a very big deal, so after a few days it just went off their radar."

"I see." Tom said. "Well, Ralph I appreciate you telling us the story and thank you for the iced tea. I guess we'll be getting along now. Sure has been nice talking with you again."

"So where are you headed from here?" Ralph asked as he rose to shake Tom's hand.

"Well we are actually headed for Canada, but we thought we would go the scenic route through Cape Vincent, and then on up through Clayton, and maybe to Alexandrea Bay, then on to the 1000 Island Bridge into Canada."

"Remember when you pulled into the driveway I asked if you were looking for directions to get to Cape Vincent?"

"Oh yeah, I know the way Ralph", Tom answered. "Just go back out to the main drag and continue on across the Limestone Bridge, and that will take you right into the Cape, right?"

"Wrong", Ralph answered. "This is why I have a lot of people stop here and ask how to get to Cape Vincent. You see, Tom, when that earthquake happened it damaged the undergirding of the Limestone Bridge. State officials shut it down for safety reasons.

'It took a while but a construction company finally came in here and started to tear down the bridge and build a new one. However, they only got about halfway through tearing it down when the company apparently went bankrupt!

'Because of the fact that little traffic comes through here anymore, there never has been a company that wanted to complete the job for fear that they would never get their money out of it.

'So the bridge still remains closed! You will have to go back out the other way about four miles and you will turn left on Highway 317. Follow that for another four miles, and turn left on East London Road. That will take you across the Limestone River and eventually you will wind up in Cape Vincent. It is quite a ways out of the way, but it is the closest way to get to Cape Vincent from here."

"Really", Tom said surprised. "Ralph, would you like to go for a ride with us? I would like to take a look at that bridge. I told you I was a bridge designer. Maybe my company can rebuild that bridge for Limestone. What do you say?"

"Sure. I don't have anything else pressing right now. Let's go!"

Tom drove down to the old bridge site. He parked and the three of them walked over to the edge of the embankment. After taking several minutes to survey the situation, Tom replied:

"You know, Ralph, I believe that we can do the job of building a new bridge for this town. I would guess that one reason that there is not much traffic coming through here is because people have learned that the bridge is out, and they automatically go elsewhere to get across the river.

'If we can build a new bridge, think how this could boost the traffic and the economy of this town. Why, we might even see Limestone come back to life! It is exciting just for me to think about it!"

"Wow that would be great", Ralph said. "Do you really think you can do it?"

"Well, I will draw up a plan and design a new bridge and present it to our upper echelon. If I can get it approved I think we will be in business.

'It is worth a shot. It sure would be nice to see Limestone back the way it once was."

"Boy, I sure would like to see that", Ralph replied. "I have lived here in this town all my life, but it never has been the same since '78. A new bridge just might be the answer. Let me know if you can pull this off, will you?"

"Absolutely; I will get to work on it as soon as I get back home. When I know something, I'll let you know."

As Tom was driving Ralph back home, his mind was already swirling about design ideas that he thought might make this project become a reality.

24

After their vacation was over, Tom went to work feverously working on a bridge design that would be appropriate for the project. He also included building costs, such as materials, labor, and equipment necessary to do the job. Several weeks later he was ready to present it to Stanley Brown, one of the owners of the company.

He knocked and entered the boss' office one morning. "Good morning Liz", Tom greeted Brown's secretary. "I believe Mr. Brown is expecting me. I have already called and got an appointment with him this morning."

"Of course, Tom; I'll let him know you are here", Liz replied. She buzzed her boss on the intercom, "Tom Chaimberbrook is here to see you Sir."

"Ah, yes; please send him in", a pleasant voice on the other end answered.

"Good morning, Sir", Tom said, greeting his superior with an extended hand as he entered Brown's office.

"And a good morning to you as well, Tom", Brown said cheerfully, arising to shake Tom's hand.

'So you have a new project that you want me to take a look at, is that right?"

"Yes Sir, I do", Tom explained reaching into his briefcase for the blueprints and plans for the proposed bridge.

Tom placed them on Brown's desk and said, "I've been working on this project for about six weeks or so.

'I feel like this is something that we can consider doing, Sir. I'll let you look it over and tell me what you think of it."

"Alright; ah huh, ah huh; I like the design, Tom; very nice work."

"Thank you, Sir. As you can see I have also worked up a reasonable calculation as to what I feel we could build this bridge for; materials, labor costs, etc."

"Yes; ah huh, ah huh; just give me a few minutes to take a good look at this and I will give you my opinion"

"Very well, Sir; take all the time you need."

As Tom waited for his boss to look over his plans, he sifted through some of the alternate plans he had in his briefcase on other projects that he had designed. He was hoping that Brown would like his original proposal however, because in his mind (Tom's) this was some of the best work that he had ever done.

After a few minutes, Brown responded, "I like the proposal, Tom. However I am a little concerned about your estimated cost of the project.

'You are pretty close on the cost of the materials and labor, but I don't see a whole lot of room for profit to the company here. Can you explain this a little further?"

"Well Sir, you see this is a personal project of mine that I would like to see come to fruition. The fact of the matter is that the small town of Limestone probably cannot come up with the funding for such a project as this. However, I feel that there is a good possibility that they could get some support from the State of New York on this because it would create a direct route to Cape Vincent without going around a 12 mile detour which is the current situation."

"Tom, I think you understand that we are in business to make a profit. When I say profit, I am not talking about a few hundred dollars. We have to operate on a much larger scale than that. If we are not making a few thousand on a given project, it would not take long for us to go out of business."

"I understand that, Sir. May I ask you a question?"

"Certainly."

"Are you satisfied with the work that I do for this company?"

"Absolutely; Tom, you are the best designer I have. You have made the company very profitable since you came here. I am proud of the work that you do."

"Thank you, Sir, I appreciate the compliment. This is why I am asking you for a favor; I am not asking for a raise, I am asking for a favor.

'You see, as I said, this is a personal matter for me. I graduated from high school in that town. I also played basketball there on a State Championship team in 1964. Unfortunately, I also lost my very best friend at the time as well.

'It happened on a cold snowy January night.

'We were playing an away game up in the Adirondack Mountains. My friend, Larry Jones was his name, had previously asked our coach if he could drive to the game because his family was celebrating his grandmother's 70th birthday. He assured Coach that he would be there in time for the varsity game.

'Coach didn't like the idea of any of his players driving to games, but he made an exception this time due to Larry's request and the fact that he had thoughts that the game may be postposed anyways due to the weather.

'The weather was fine earlier in the day, but it started snowing again on our way up into the mountains. Larry never showed up for the game.

'On our way back to Limestone after the game, we ran across a bad accident. We soon found out it was Larry's car that was involved. He had slid off the icy road and hit a tree.

'They rushed Larry to a hospital in Watertown, about an hour or so away. The doctor did all he could to save Larry. He had multiple broken ribs and extensive internal bleeding. He died about an hour later.

'I would like to build this bridge as a memorial to Larry. I believe that we can get the funding from the State to help, but they probably will not go for much more than what I have proposed."

"I see, ah huh, ah huh" Brown responded. Well, I'll tell you what, Tom that was a compelling story. And because it is YOU, I will make an exception to what I would ordinarily not approve of. However, you are still going to have to get this past my partner Gerald Wilkinson. Frankly, he may not be as easily persuaded as I was."

"I understand, Sir. Thank you for understanding where I am coming from."

"As you know, Gerald has a temporary office set up in New York right now, to oversee the bridge project we have going over the lower section of the Hudson River."

"Yes sir, I believe my colleague Ken Shaharly designed that bridge,"

"That is correct. Now I will contact Gerald and set up an appointment for you to meet with him. As soon as I know something, I'll let you know."

"Thank you Sir", Tom said as he arose from his chair and started gathering his papers and putting them back in his briefcase. "I will do my best to convince Mr. Wilkinson".

"Ah huh, ah huh; well don't be too surprised if he turns you down. Gerald is a real businessman. He can be a tough nut to crack sometimes. Good luck!"

"Thank you, Sir"

The two shook hands and Tom left Brown's office. He had in mind to call Ralph Stevens and let him know how his meeting had gone with one of his bosses. But on second thought, he decided to wait until after he had talked to Wilkinson.

Later that evening...........

BUZZZZ! The phone was ringing.

"Honey, will you get that", Lori shouted from the kitchen. "My hands are full here getting supper ready".

"Sure", Tom answered, getting up out of his favorite living room chair. He went to the phone and picked it up.

"Hello?" he answered curiously.

"Good evening, Tom", came the voice on the other end of the line. "Stanley Brown here, hope I'm not disturbing anything?"

"Not at all, Sir; what's up?"

"I got in touch with Gerald Wilkinson and he wants to see you in his New York office at 8:00 AM this coming Tuesday morning. I have made arrangements for you to fly to New York Monday afternoon and have got hotel reservations for you at The Paramount Hotel. Be at the airport at 2:00 pm Monday afternoon and pick up your tickets at the ticket counter. Good luck!"

"Thank you so much, Mr. Brown. I deeply appreciate this."

"You are welcome, Tom. Have a good evening!"

"Oh, I will. You have already made my day."

Tom hung up the phone and Lori asked, "Well, you seem happy all of the sudden, who was that?"

"Mr. Brown; he has made an appointment for me with Mr. Wilkinson to see if I can get my design and project approved."

"Ah, you won't have any trouble getting it approved, dear. You are pretty convincing when you want to be."

"Well I don't know about this one. Mr. Brown warned that Mr. Wilkinson can be hard to convince sometimes. But we will see."

"Alright; supper is ready, let's eat."

"Ummm, sure does smell good. I am hungry, and blessed to have a wonderful wife like you."

25

Tuesday Morning, September 11, 2001.......

Tom was up bright and early. He had not slept all that well due to his mind whirling about how to present his plan to Gerald Wilkinson. But he got up and showered, dressed in a nice suit, and headed down stairs from his hotel room.

He grabbed a quick bite to eat and cup of coffee and headed out the door. He summoned a taxi and climbed in.

"Where to, Bud?" the driver asked.

"World Trade Center, Number One Tower", Tom answered.

Traffic was heavy as the taxi made its way through lower Manhattan. It was a beautiful sunny day, clear skies with the temperature nearing mid-60 on its way to the low 70's later in the day.

The taxi driver got Tom to his destination at 7:45 AM. He paid the cabbie and entered through large front entrance of the Number One Tower, heading straight for the elevators.

He pressed the button for the 84th floor, and the elevator started to slowly ascend. It took a few minutes to reach his floor, as the elevator stopped several times on the way up to let off other people who were scurrying to get to work on time.

The elevator finally reached the 84th floor. Tom stepped off and headed straight down the hall two corridors, turned left and stopped at the second door on the right. The sign on the door read: Temporary office of BROWN and WILKINSON Bridge Contractors.

Tom glanced at his watch, precisely 8:00 AM! He entered with a smile on his face and confidence in his step.

"May I help you Sir?" the receptionist asked as Tom approached the front desk.

"Yes Madam", Tom answered. "I'm Tom Chaimberbrook, and I have an appointment this morning with Mr. Wilkinson."

"Of course", the receptionist answered with a smile. "I let him know you are here"

She reached for the intercom, "Mr. Tom Chaimberbrook is here to see you Mr. Wilkinson."

"Great, send him in right away", came the reply.

Tom entered Wilkinson's office with a smile and extended his hand. "Great to see you again Mr. Wilkinson, it has been awhile since we have talked."

Wilkinson arose from his desk chair and reached for Tom's hand. "Tom, it is good to see you again. Hope all is well with your family?"

"Oh yes Sir. Everyone is fine. And how are you doing?"

"Doing very, well, thank you; my wife has been a little under the weather lately, but she is feeling better now."

"I'm glad to hear that Sir. So how are we coming along with the Hudson River project?"

"It is getting near completion actually. We are hoping to be finished here in another couple of months or so. I'm looking forward to getting back to Kansas. As the saying goes, 'New York is a nice place to visit, but I don't want to live here'"

"I hear you, Sir. 'There is no place like home', as another saying goes."

"So, Stanley tells me that you have a project that you want to show me. Is that correct?"

"Yes Sir", Tom answered opening up his briefcase and pulling out his design and calculations. "It is all right there, Sir. Take a good look at it and tell me what you think."

Wilkinson spread out the paperwork on his desk and began sifting through it. "Very impressive design, Tom; You always do great work, this looks really good."

"Thank you, Sir. I appreciate the compliment."

"Now let's take a look at your figures. It will take me a few minutes."

"Take all the time you need, Sir. I'll just take a look at the view from up here if you don't mind?"

"Not at all, the view is quite spectacular as you can see."

"Wow, it sure is dazzling", Tom agreed as he looked out the skyscraper window. "You can literally see for miles from up here."

"Yes, I have enjoyed this view since I've been here", Wilkinson replied while still gazing at Tom's papers. "But I'm anxious now to get back home."

"I understand, Sir. Wow, this is pretty exciting for me. I've never been in the World Trade Center before. I can even see the Statue of Liberty from here!"

A few minutes later........

Tom was still looking out the window as Wilkinson was still looking through the paperwork Tom had prepared.

"Being up this high almost makes you feel like you are above the clouds!" Tom exclaimed. "Except there aren't any clouds today; are we in a flight path here Mr. Wilkinson?"

"Flight path; No I don't believe so. Why do you ask?"

"Well it just looks like a large plane is coming straight at this building. I thought maybe we might be in a flight path of some kind."

"What?" Wilkinson jerked his head up and looked out the window where Tom was standing.

"Oh my God!" Wilkinson shouted. "That is a plane headed right at us. Run Tom, head for cover! Dive! Dive! Dive!"

AND THEN THE PLANE HIT!!!!!!

*THE BRICKS HAVE FALLEN
DOWN
BUT WE WILL REBUILD
WITH DRESSED STONE;
THE FIG TREES HAVE
BEEN FELLED
BUT WE WILL REPLACE
THEM
WITH CEDARS.*

ISAIAH 9:10

Part

Three

Sixteen Years Later

July 2017

26

One might ask...What ever happened to Limestone and the characters that were in the story? Glad you asked! Here is a brief synonymous of what happened.

LORI CHAIMBERBROOK

Lori was completely devastated after the loss of her husband on that fateful day of 9/11. She suffered deep depression for almost a year after words, partaking of many anti-depressants to help calm her nerves and help her function in a somewhat normal lifestyle.

With the help of her grown children she was able to get her life back on track. Two years after that tragic day, she sold their home in Kansas and moved to Woodstock, Georgia to be near her ageing parents Marvin and Sandy Smith. One year later her youngest daughter and husband also moved to Georgia along with their two young children.

But tragedy struck again a year later.

Marv, who seemed to be in excellent health for his age of 80 years, was out on his regular daily routine one morning, jogging around the block where they lived. Upon returning to the house, he told Sandy that he felt a little tired and he was going to lie down for a few minutes.

After an hour, Sandy went to check on him in the bedroom. She found him dead! The Coroner later determined that he had died from a massive heart attack.

Lori never remarried, stating that the only man that she ever truly loved was Tom Chaimberbrook.

Today at age 73, she spends most of her time reading books, reminiscing the good old days with her mother (now 92), and occasionally going on a shopping spree now and then. She frequently stays in touch with Tom's parents, but seldom visits them anymore at their Texas home.

THOMAS and MARTHA CHAIMBERBROOK

Thomas and Martha are both 93 years old now, and still in remarkably good health. They sold their home just outside Corpus Christi, Texas five years ago and are now living in a comfortable two bedroom apartment in the Dallas area.

They enjoy their leisurely time hosting old time friends whom Thomas used to work with. Occasionally will take in a movie or go see a live play. Thomas even goes to the driving range every so often and hits a few golf balls, but is unable to actually get out on the course and play the game.

They mourned over Tom's death for a long time as well. For a few years, they even went to New York on the 9/11 anniversary in remembrance of their son.

Through all of this, they met others that were tragically affected by 9/11. They started up a bereavement foundation for local families in the Texas area that had lost loved ones on that day. Thomas became the head prayer warrior of that organization. With his help and counseling, many families and individuals were comforted through their grief.

Every once in a while Thomas still gets a call from someone asking for prayer support, which he is always more than willing to provide.

The frequent phone calls from Lori keep them going. They are always anxious to hear from her. Their grandchildren that live in Kansas will visit occasionally. Thomas and Martha look forward to each one of their visits, and always welcome them with open arms.

LAWRENCE and IRENE JONES

Lawrence struggled for many months after the tragic death of their son Larry. He was on a very heavy anti-depressant medicine, but his nerves were about shot.

He struggled on his job, not being able to concentrate. After several warnings from his employer for inferior job performance, he was let go. His employer was gracious enough to give him a layoff slip, allowing Lawrence to draw unemployment.

A year went by, and every time Lawrence and Irene went to a basketball game to watch their younger son Tommy play, Lawrence would ultimately have the memories of Larry come back, and this would result in another breakdown.

Unable to cope with the situation any longer, the family put their home up for sale and moved to Florida to get away from all the memories that haunted Lawrence. The move was the answer, as Lawrence finally was able to get his mind focused and was able to get back to a normal lifestyle.

Tommy continued his basketball career in Florida, and had an outstanding senior year. After his graduation he enrolled at Grossman State University, where he hoped to play for Marvin Smith. However that never transpired. Marvin had already accepted a job as assistant coach with the Kentucky Colonels of the new ABA.

Tommy did, however, play at Grossman for a couple of years, but gave it up after his sophomore year to concentrate on his classes, ultimately earning a teaching degree and is still teaching advanced mathematics at a junior college in Florida. (He also coaches basketball.)

Lawrence and Irene, both in their early 90's now, live in a nice retirement development just south of Orlando. Lawrence still plays an occasional round of golf, and both go to the 'Y' almost every day. They are in good health and are enjoying the twilight of their years.

RICK JACKSON and NATHAN BOONE

Neither Rick nor Nathan was recruited to play basketball after high school, but both were determined to play somewhere. So they both enrolled at Yale University where they made the team as walk-ons.

Both studied law and earned a Bachelor's Degree and later finished their Masters at Harvard.

After graduation, they went in together and formed their own law firm: **Jackson, Boone, and Associates.** The firm was very successful their first few years in Boston, Massachusetts.

In 1991 they moved the firm to New York and set up shop in the World Trade Center Tower Number Two. They hired several more attorneys into their firm and business exploded! Rick and Nathan were running one of the most powerful law firms in the country!

Then, of course, came September 11, 2001! Rick was killed that day as he was making his way down from the 78th floor when the second plane hit Tower Number Two.

Nathan was not in the building that day. In fact he was in Philadelphia, Pennsylvania representing a corporation that was being sued for income tax evasion. (Boone actually won that case and beat the Federal Government!)

But Nathan was so depressed and shattered by his lifelong friend's death that he couldn't carry on. He turned the reigns of the corporation over to his Chief of Operations and retired a couple of years later.

Nathan and his wife Donna now live in a small cottage house on Long Island.

VIDAL HOLBROOK

Vidal became the star of the Limestone basketball team after Tom Chaimberbrook graduated. Playing his final two years under Coach Thomas Chaimberbrook, Vidal played better with each game.

His senior year was just sensational as he destroyed every rebounding record in the Conference and averaged 27 points per game on top of that.

Fred Lewis at Syracuse University recruited Vidal heavily, even coming to watch him play three or four times. But Vidal didn't want to play locally; he wanted to be in with the elite crowd.

After being turned down at Duke University, he finally decided to go to UCLA and play for the legendary John Wooden. He had a mediocre career at UCLA, but never made it to the pros.

Disheartened by not being able to play professional basketball, Vidal began a life of partying. He started drinking heavily, got into drugs, was arrested a few times for drunk driving, and finally was sentenced for two years for driving while intoxicated and with a suspended license.

He was paroled after serving a one year sentence for good behavior. A friend helped him get a job, and he got his life straightened out for about a year or so.

He met a nice young woman and they were getting pretty serious about getting married. But one evening Vidal decided to stop in at a local bar and just have one beer to relax after a hard day's work.

That one beer led to another, then another, and still another. After several, he had to have 'one more for the road'. The bartender offered to drive him back to his apartment, but Vidal insisted that he was alright and proceeded out the door.

The truth of the matter was that Vidal was so drunk that he could barely walk to his car. When he started back to his apartment, he was so disoriented that he wasn't even sure where he was going. He was weaving all over the road.

Then he looked in his rear view mirror and noticed red lights behind him. For fear of being stopped again for driving while intoxicated, he stepped on the gas to get away from the oncoming police officer.

After hitting speeds in excess of 90 MPH, Vidal lost control of his vehicle. He swerved right, and then left before going across the road and down an embankment and hitting a large tree at somewhere around 70 MPH!

Vidal met the LORD that day, one week shy of his 27th birthday.

27

And then, of course, there is the question of, What ever happened to Limestone? ……….

Well, Limestone today isn't even a mere speck on the map. With a population of only a dozen or so, there are no businesses, no churches, no post office, and no schools, no anything really! Just a spot in the road where there once was a lively town. Far gone from yesteryear, not even memories are left there anymore.

That is unless you happen to be heading down that road and are not sure where you are going. You may want to swing into the driveway at 22 North Road. There you will find an elderly man rocking back and forth in his rocking chair on his front porch.

Yep, Ralph Stevens still lives there in Limestone. Ralph once said: "Limestone is where I was born, and Limestone is where I will die!"

Upon pulling into his driveway, the first thing Ralph might say may be: "Hello there stranger. Are you looking for directions to Cape Vincent?"

Of course, Ralph is always obliging to give you directions, but if you are not in any hurry, he would love to have you sit down for a while and listen to the story about how Limestone used to be.

Oh, he will tell you all about that great basketball teams that Limestone had back in the 1960's, especially the one they had back in '64 when Limestone won the State Championship!

He will talk about Tom Chaimberbrook, the greatest high school basketball player ever to play the game (in Ralph's mind). Then he will proceed to tell you about the two teams that followed that Championship season. Both made it to the Northern Regional where they once again met their arch-rival Adirondack Parochial, and lost!

He may even go back further in time, to the late 30's and early 40's. That was when he played at Limestone High and played with great players such as Marvin Smith and Thomas Chaimberbrook.

"I want to tell you", Ralph would say, "That Marvin Smith had the best set shot I have ever seen! And Thomas Chaimberbrook had a tremendous hook shot that was unstoppable!"

You might then ask, "What is a set shot?"

"Oh, well, that was an old timey shot back in those days; you probably don't remember anything like that." Ralph would try to explain.

After telling the story of Limestone's great basketball history, and if you were still interested to learn more, Ralph then would go on to tell you all about the earthquake of '78 and the ensuing fire that destroyed the town.

Yes, you could learn a lot about Limestone from Ralph Stevens if you had the time and were eager to listen. Even at age 93, his memory is a sharp as ever, and he is literally a living history book!

Then, after you have spent the better part of a day listening to his stories, Ralph will get around to giving you those directions to Cape Vincent that you stopped to ask about in the first place! He will tell you about the 12 mile detour that you have to take to get across the Limestone River, because, you see, the LARRY JONES MEMORIAL BRIDGE that Tom Chaimberbrook wanted to build never came to fruition.

After the 9/11 attack and after losing both his partner in business, Gerald Wilkinson, and his best designer, in Tom Chaimberbrook, Stanley Brown was shaken to the core. He hung on until the current jobs that the company was working on were completed, including the lower Hudson River Bridge project.

Then, after 36 years in the bridge construction business, he sold the company to a large bridge contractor in San Francisco, California. The Larry Jones project was forgotten, but the remains of the old bridge are still visible today.

Ralph Stevens spends most of his time on his front porch now, watching the birds and squirrels play around the many bird feeders that he has around his house.

He loves to reminisce about 'The Good Old Days' and it brings a smile to his face. Of course, there were plenty of bad memories in Ralph's life as well, but he tries not to think about those memories very much. He would rather think about the more pleasant ones.

Because there is one thing that Ralph Stevens has learned in his 93 years of living, and that is:

LIFE IS WHAT IT IS!